The
Ben Calder
Story

The
BEN CALDER
Story

Stephen Zeifman

TORONTO

Exile Editions
2005

First published in Canada in 2005 by
Exile Editions Ltd.
20 Dale Avenue
Toronto, Ontario, M4W 1K4
telephone: 416 485 9468
www.ExileEditions.com

This is a work of fiction. Names, characters, places and incidents are
the product of the author's imagination or are used fictitiously, and
any resemblance to actual persons, living or dead, events, or locales is
entirely coincidental.

Library and Archives Canada Cataloguing in Publication

Zeifman, Stephen

    The Ben Calder story / Stephen Zeifman.

ISBN 1-55096-643-X

    I. Title.

PS8599.E35B45 2005   C813'.54   C2005-906502-8

Design and Composition: Michael P.M. Callaghan
Cover: Stephen Zeifman
Typesetting: Moons of Jupiter
Printed in Canada: Gauvin Imprimerie

The publisher would like to acknowledge the financial assistance of
The Canada Council for the Arts.

Conseil des Arts   Canada Council
du Canada   for the Arts

Sales Distribution:
McArthur & Company c/o Harper Collins
1995 Markham Road, Toronto, ON M1B 5M8
toll free: 1 800 387 0117   (fax) 1 800 668 5788

for

Ruth and Lou

Contents

PROLOGUE

⊙✦⊙

The Sabbath

It was a Saturday morning in July. Ben Calder was six years old
walking along a country road with his father. They were going
to synagogue. Ben was wearing grey wool shorts, a white short-
sleeved shirt with an open collar, knee socks and black oxford
shoes. His father wore a dark suit and tie and a pork-brim straw
fedora with a turquoise blue cotton hatband. It was well over
ninety degrees and the tar was melting beneath their feet. Ben
was holding his father's hand and they were rushing, already a
few minutes late for the morning service. Ben was a step behind
his father and trying to keep up.

The air was still and smelled of pine sap and creosote. On
their left were dense areas of woodlot that blocked the breeze
coming in off the lake. Every hundred yards, though, a conces-
sion road cut through the trees to the water and the lakefront
lots. On their right was a row of cottages facing the road. These
were rental properties and stood in constant shade. The occu-
pants had to use the public beach a half mile away. People took
these places by the week or the month and some returned year
after year but Ben never got to know any of the kids who stayed
there.

Ben hated going to morning services, hated dressing up on a Saturday, hated having to stand still amongst the men with their bad breath and scuffed shoes, but he liked walking with his father, who arrived every Friday night and left on Sunday after dinner. There was something elusive about his father and Ben liked to pin him down with this physical contact.

The synagogue was in a cottage that the congregation rented for the summer. It sat alone in a field across the road from the Tides Hotel. It was a wooden building, grey and weathered, badly in need of a coat of paint, with a screened-in porch and a front door facing east. Some guests at the hotel would give up shuffleboard and badminton, the generous weekend breakfast buffet and come across the road for the service. All the windows were opened and there were about sixteen men of varying age, from twenty to eighty, who were *davening* when Ben and his father arrived. They all wore *taluses* and dark suits and in the shaded room the black and white contrasts were striking, like Borduas juxtaposed with Rothko, in a constant rocking motion. On their heads the men wore skullcaps, fedoras, or an odd assortment of plaid, paisley, and seersucker summer caps. The davening was like muttering in a vaguely musical way, with each man reading at his own pace saying the occasional word clearly and out loud. A member of the congregation, neither a rabbi nor a cantor, was leading the service. Behind him was a small Ark, a free-standing cupboard, covered with a blue velvet curtain decorated with two lions embroidered in gold thread. The Ark held the Torah.

Ben was the only child in the room. His friends, with cottages near by, were all Jewish but their parents were no longer religious or observant so they didn't have to come. They went fishing instead or played on the beach. Ben's mother was not religious either but his father was and in these matters he had to do what his father wanted. He was already bored and moved away from the group to stand and look out the window. There were cicadas and crows and the sound of a big Shepherd motor launch racing across the bay.

Ben's grandfather had built their cottage in 1941, on a long narrow lot outside of Jackson's Point, and being a deeply religious man he helped found this congregation. Most Sundays he went from cottage to cottage collecting money from people in the community to make sure that it survived. His grandfather was born in Poland and came to Canada as a young man in 1919. He carried a package of Charms in his pocket at all times and this morning he led Ben back to his seat with the promise of candy. Charms had a unique flavour, more fruity and less sweet than Life Savers, and they were square, with a little indentation, so you could work at it with your tongue until there was a hole all the way through. Ben did this for the next fifteen minutes.

When it was time to take out the Torah he sang with the other members of the group, it was his favourite song, but he did not reach over to touch the Torah as it passed held high by one of the men. When the song was over he fell silent again and stared at the pages of his book. He had been going to Hebrew school five times a week for almost two years and he could read the language but he didn't understand a word. It would continue like that until he was a teenager.

There was a little stand, selling ice cream cones, pop, penny candy and Lucky Elephant popcorn on the same property as the synagogue. It was a solid wooden structure, facing the road, with flip-up shutters that hinged and hooked on the roof. It had a white arborite counter that the owners cleaned with vinegar. Ben would walk to the stand at least once a day to buy a treat and give his mother some relief. No one worried about a six-year-old boy alone on the roads then. When the service was over the men talked and folded their prayer shawls. Some spoke in English, others in Yiddish. They gossiped and joked and talked about the latest news from Israel. The screen door opened and slammed shut as each person left. There would be no treat from the stand on the way home. It was Saturday and the Orthodox didn't carry money on the Sabbath.

Later Ben and his sister Hannah, who were the only grandchildren, would have to sit through a long lunch until they were allowed to go to the beach. This week their aunt and uncle were visiting from Paris and every meal was an occasion. Sidney Calder was a medical student with an interest in Freud and somewhere between the Yeshiva in New York, where he started his post-secondary education, and the Sorbonne, where he finished it, he had renounced God. This was a great disappointment to his father. In the morning, instead of going to services, Sid and his wife Nola had gone sailing and just made it back in time for lunch. She put a shirt on over her bikini, the latest thing from France, and sat down at the table with an adoring glance at Sid and a robust laugh. Mrs. Calder senior, Ben's step-grandmother, a recent addition to the family, looked at Nola without affection, and waited for her husband to bless the bread before beginning to eat. Ben's grandfather had waited fourteen months to remarry after his wife of thirty years, who was also his first cousin and had travelled to Toronto from Poland with him, had passed away. Orthodox Jewish men needed a woman around, a wife, someone to prepare the Sabbath. It was not the most elevated reason for marriage and they often made mistakes.

Also present at the table were Ben's nineteen-year-old uncle, Morris, his father's youngest brother, and his recently announced fiancée, Faye.

There was leftover chicken, brisket, lima beans, and a potato pudding that had been baking in the oven since Friday morning. It was brown and crisp with a thick crust on the outside and grey and mushy inside. With this dish there was a legitimate concern about waiting an hour after eating before going in the water. The women served the food and cleared the table, did the dishes and brought out dessert. The men ate and talked and said grace at the end of the meal.

Ben was allowed to leave then and went to his room. He changed into a bathing suit, opened the back door and headed for the beach, with his mother calling after him not to go into the water until she got there. He couldn't swim at all and waited for her on a large smooth rock, one of three or four that were an aspect of their beach. There was a light on-shore breeze kicking up waves about a foot high that broke with a rhythmic regularity. It was a sound he would never forget. A lake was like a small animal with a beating heart compared to the relaxed undulating rhythm of the sea.

His mother came down carrying a bowl of fruit with Morris and Faye beside her and Hannah following close behind. His mother, in a blue bathing suit, was a dark-haired beauty with a great body and a movie-star smile. She was twenty-six that summer, tanned and fit.

Ben watched her put the fruit down on a small table and pull a white wooden chaise into the sun. Morris came over and mussed his hair and when his mother sat down and put a bathing cap on Hannah, Ben walked into the water. He stood about waist-deep facing the horizon then turned and, with his hands on the bottom and his feet out behind him, crawled toward the shore with the waves breaking over his back. He put his face in the water, he floated, he blew bubbles, but he didn't swim. Morris tried to show him how but Ben ignored him and sat at the edge of the beach, piling stones into towers. Hannah ran back and forth in front of him, trying to avoid the waves. She was three.

The previous day Ben's mother had banished him from her bath. It had come as a shock. Since infancy he had bathed with her and yesterday she kicked him out. Just like that. No more. He was fascinated by her tan lines and focused on the contrast between her dark skin and her white breasts with their large nipples floating in front of him as he sat down, in the tub, facing her, between her legs. But there must have been something in his gaze that day, something not quite childlike, something that touched his mother, making her feel his presence as a boy, and that was the end. From then on, if he wanted to see women naked he would have to find a picture, go to a strip show, or learn how to make them feel comfortable enough in his presence to take off their clothes.

He watched his mother stand up, glistening with sweat after lying in the hot sun, and tuck her hair into a white bathing cap before wading into the water for a swim. She swam straight out about a hundred and fifty yards from shore, to depths he couldn't even imagine, grown-up depths, with a stylish crawl stroke, before turning and swimming back. She was smiling and her eyes shone as well. She was irresistible. And Morris didn't notice when Faye came to stand beside him while he and Ben watched Helen, Ben's mother, take off her bathing cap and shake her black shoulder-length hair loose before lying down again on the chaise.

Ben's grandfather came down to the beach then carrying an old army cot. It was his cot. Faded unbleached canvas on a weathered wood frame. He surveyed the scene and chose a place away from the others, high up on the beach, to open the cot. He smiled at his grandchildren and lay down before closing his eyes to the sun and sleeping for almost an hour. For him, not a frivolous man, it was stolen time that he folded close to his chest.

Sid and Nola had followed behind him with Sid mocking his father's particular bowlegged stride. Ben tried not to laugh because it was so silly, such an obvious and exaggerated impersonation but Hannah started to move just like Sid, tummy out, walking on the sides of her feet. Ben's father arrived just then and thought she was impersonating him. He was skinny as a dandelion but there was no denying his legs were somewhat bowed.

Everyone laughed, and the three brothers raced into the water and swam to a dock three cottages away. Ben's father was the first one back by half a length, followed by Sid, then Morris twenty yards behind. They'd been doing the same thing since they were kids. There was about them a bond that was unspoken and close. None of them had yet recovered from the loss of their mother. She died at forty-six.

As the afternoon passed, friends from nearby cottages and some relatives in the vicinity came to visit. The women sat with each other, knitting and talking. A tray of cold beers arrived along with fruit, cake and nuts. Ben's dad and two friends played three-corner catch across the beach with a football, trying not wake the old man. Ben watched it all and pushed Hannah into the water when he got bored. She cried and he was made to sit on the lawn by himself until he could behave.

FAMILY LIFE

In time his parents stopped getting along. They had cultural differences. His mother, Helen, was of Russian-Jewish descent from a wealthy non-religious family in northern Ontario. She was one of three sisters and a brother who'd moved down to Toronto as teenagers, into a big Tudor-style house on Austin Crescent, in the shadow of Casa Loma, with a view of the city below. The belles of Oakwood Collegiate, the Penny girls, lived with their mother. Their absentee father would leave his mistress and his store in Cochrane to come down and see them on his way to a card game in New York.

Ben's father, Ira, was the child of Polish immigrants, cabinetmakers in the old country, furriers in the new. They were Orthodox Jews and his grandmother still swung chickens around her head in the kitchen, on Friday afternoons, saying a prayer before butchering them out in the yard on Euclid Street. There were carp in the bathtub to bake for dinner, wine vats in the cellar, and the family insisted Helen go to the *mickva* for cleansing before her wedding to Ira. The *mickva* was a dank pool that revolted her. She never recovered.

Ten years later it was: "You low-class Polish bastard, spineless shit who can't crawl out from under your father and make a real living."

"Arrogant Russian bitch. Where do you get off talking to me like that? Your fucking father pissed away a fortune on gambling and whores."

"Creep. You have no right to talk about my father like that."

"Cunt, I'll talk about that free-loading has-been any way I want."

"I hate your fuckin' guts. I curse myself every day for ending up with a nothing schmuck when I could have had any man I wanted."

By then Ben had another sister, Connie. She was eight years younger and shared a bedroom with Hannah. Ben's room was beside his parents and he often lay awake at night listening to them dissecting each other with language honed on a strop of frustration and disappointment. And sometimes, when the yelling stopped, there was lovemaking that caused the bed to squeal and the headboard to bang into the wall. Ben lay still on his back, his head riven from another migraine, moaning until someone came, his mother or father, to put a cold compress on his forehead and tell him everything was going to be alright.

His parents' fighting became chronic and routine. The words were awful and the sound of them was worse but they lost their power to shock. And then everything stopped. There was an unnatural quiet in the house. His mother radiated warmth and affection. His father was attentive to all. Even Connie got bounced in the air and jiggled on his knee.

Ben was eleven. His family was spending a lot of time with other families and their kids. On Sundays they got together for barbecues or Chinese food or they all went to a movie and out for something to eat afterward. The kids played together and the parents talked and drank cocktails. These were new friends, wealthier and not at all religious although they were all from Jewish backgrounds. The men were doctors, lawyers, builders, men of means, buying houses in Forest Hill Village. They were not men like Ira, who dropped out of school to get married and go into business with his father. It was something Helen never let him forget.

Dr. Harold Bloom, a surgeon at Mount Sinai, and his family were always in the picture and some days, after summer vacation began, Ben would spend an afternoon with his mother and Dr. Bloom just driving around in the car. They'd go to small towns and look in antique stores and there was talk and laughter and Dr. Bloom made a point of including Ben in conversations and in games, like Botticelli, they played on the road. It was the first summer in three years that Ben didn't go to overnight camp, and the family spent weekends at the cottage and had plans to spend the month of August there as well. The Blooms had rented a place just down the beach.

A few weeks into the summer, on a Tuesday morning, Ben came out of the washroom and passed by his mother's bedroom. The door was closed and Ben's mother was on the phone. Something in the sound of her voice got his attention. It was like she was trying not to be heard talking to her sister, Rose, the crazy one, who'd had a breakdown and was given shock treatments after the birth of her second child. She had only been out of the hospital a week. Ben heard his mother say,

"I'm going to leave Ira . . . In the fall . . . Harold loves me . . . Of course I love him. He's the first man I've ever loved . . . He'll leave her . . . He promised . . . I'm not that stupid . . . I'll take the kids with me. Ira never wanted them anyway . . . I can say that. Trust me. The selfish bastard . . . Harold is very good with Ben . . . Yes. Ben likes him very much . . . It's not just about sex . . . Oh, your ideas are so out of whack . . . I know you're my older sister. I know what I'm doing . . . I'll tell him when I'm good and ready."

It was a conversation he wished he'd never heard. It shattered his world. He spent days and nights thinking about Harold Bloom and his father. Comparing them, asking himself which one would be better to live with. Harold Bloom, he decided, meant nothing to him and his father meant everything. In the darkness of his room, late into the night, he tried to figure out how he could kill Harold Bloom with his BB gun. Ben would have to shove the barrel into Harold's eye and fire into his brain.

He was never comfortable with Harold Bloom again and acted badly whenever he and his mother were alone with him. She sent Ben to a day camp for the last two weeks in July to get rid of him. Day camp then was strictly for losers. Kids who couldn't cut it away from home. They were bed wetters, nose pickers, fussy eaters, kids with health problems and disabilities, not the kind of kids he was used to hanging out with. It didn't matter, he went until they moved up to the cottage in August. At the day camp he won every athletic prize there was. It was a joke. At school he never won anything.

In the fall, on an otherwise regular weeknight after dinner, Ben's father tore the dining-room curtains down — ripping the rod out of the ceiling, scattering plaster and screws — and yelled so loud, like a animal that had been shot beside the heart, that the walls shook and the children froze in their tracks. Ira ran out the door after that and Ben ran after him, afraid that this was the end, that he would never see his father again. Ira got into the car and Ben got in with him. His father was crying and stepped hard on the accelerator, spraying gravel in all directions as he backed out of the driveway. He drove to Bathurst Street and turned left, heading south, with no destination in mind and then stopped suddenly beside a variety store. He got out of the car and came back with a pack of cigarettes. He had never smoked and had trouble even opening the pack. Finally he lit a cigarette, took a drag and choked.

"What the fuck do people get out of these," he said, when he stopped coughing. He kept trying to smoke though but couldn't, thinking that in smoking there might be a cure for what was making him sick, a cure for having the rug pulled out from under him, from having his whole life change from a miserable truth to one big lie.

"Your mother is a fucking bitch and don't you ever forget it."

"I won't," Ben said, lighting a cigarette of his own.

His father took him home after that and Ben heard he went over to Harold Bloom's house and threatened him with a knife. He must have cared more than Ben's mother thought. She spent the next month in the hospital. Some mysterious illness that required a great deal of rest. Ben's parents wouldn't separate for another fifteen years.

SCHOOL

At school he was a child who was visible, who could not hide at the back of the class and keep his head low avoiding the teacher's attention. There was something about him, a combination of his looks and his energy that made him a target for the poisoned arrows his teachers secretly carried hidden in their quivers. His Grade Four teacher, Miss Adams, young and dark-haired, with freckles and a bright smile, well-dressed and well-mannered, who reminded him a little of his mother's other sister, Lola, would keep him in after school for misbehaving in class. She made him do chores like wash the blackboards, hang pictures and straighten up the rows of desks. She would talk to him in a sweet voice all the time he was there and then reward him for a job well done with kisses on his forehead and his cheeks and lips. He didn't like her kissing him but he thought she was just being nice. It was no worse than when his aunts or his parents' friends tried to kiss him.

In Grade Five, his teacher, Miss Wriggley, Plum Wriggley, who was tall and thin with short brownish hair, a long face and glasses, had a different agenda that he would only understand later. She would keep him in once or twice a month and she would yell at him about his talking out of turn, or leaving his seat without permission, and then she would get down on her knees, holding him by the shoulders, and she would shake him, while continuing to yell, pounding him against her bony body, on her and off her, on her and off her, until what, until she came. Then she would stand up and straighten her dress and send him home. She didn't frighten him and he knew something was going on that was not about disrupting the class, but he didn't know what. He was only nine.

At Hebrew school, which he began attending at five years of age, going Monday to Thursday from four until six, and later from six until eight, as well as Sunday morning from ten until twelve, he was loud and outspoken, totally wild and out of control. The teachers there, old men from Europe mostly, just beat him. They hit him with rulers, curtain rods, yardsticks and pointers, with whatever was available for striking out in anger. One man in particular, Mr. Kahane, liked to come up behind him when he was talking and punch him in the back of the head with a fat ring he wore on his finger. Mr. Kahane worked for his father as a mink cutter during the day and taught Hebrew in the evening. When Ben complained to his father about Mr. Kahane he was told to behave and he wouldn't get hit. There was some truth to that but it wasn't the point. It wasn't what he wanted from his father. He was just a kid, ten or eleven, not even five feet tall and he must have weighed about sixty pounds. The blows were always out of scale, too big for the slightness of his frame, so small in comparison to the size and weight of the person administering them.

Ben knew that he didn't want anything school had to offer except for the opportunity to be with his friends. And with each successive year the ways in which he was treated lessened any respect he had for those people in positions of authority. Even the principal, with his Clark Kent haircut and glasses, would whack him across the hands with the rubber strap once or twice a year. Going to elementary school for six hours a day was agony and the addition of Hebrew school was torture. By adding another two hours, of dry instruction in a language that he cared nothing about, his parents showed no consideration for the kind of person he was. To them he existed only to fulfill their needs.

In Grade Seven, junior high — the onset of adolescence, acne and spontaneous erections — Miss Leeb, his English teacher, kept him in for a talk one day after school and she started crying. She was upset because he looked at her like she was "a piece of shit." He said that wasn't his intent. In fact, he thought she was quite pretty but he was bored in class and the boredom must have shaded his expression to one that looked like contempt. She felt better after that, knowing that he liked her. She paid more attention to his written work and tried to engage him in class discussions.

He started drawing then. Drawing her from life and then as he imagined she'd look without clothes. He spent hours on the drawings, working up the form and the detail.

Mme. Bustamante, his French teacher that year, wore skin-tight dresses that looked like spandex and sat on the corner of her desk, legs crossed, skirt up, tits out, moving slowly against the desk until all the boys in the class were hard. It was in Grade Seven French that Howard Schwartz decided to become a gynecologist so he could see cunt every day, all day. It was unlikely that the French teacher ever became his patient, but many other women did. The students were certain that she wore no underwear, that she took them off before class, and Ben would draw pictures of her in high heels with her skirt up above her waist, stepping out of her panties and crumpling them into her purse. The better drawings he shared with his friends. Some hid them inside their textbook, *Cours Moyen de Français*, and would, on occasion, jerk-off in class. Mme. Bustamante was sensitive to nuance and seemed to encourage this behaviour.

Through junior high and high school nothing changed. He was often in trouble, made to stand up as an example of what the other students shouldn't do. The teachers all wanted something from him that he wouldn't or couldn't deliver.

Ben didn't want success in school nor the accolades that went with it. He didn't want to create opportunities for himself. He didn't want money or wealth or the kind of life he was surrounded with in Forest Hill Village where his family had recently moved. He didn't believe in love or the family. It seemed to him that real life was to be avoided at all costs and he pursued the things that allowed him to escape. By eighteen he was riding a motorcycle, drinking regularly, smoking. He'd tried drugs and was most comfortable lying with a girl in his arms. He was determined that his life would have no resemblance to that of his parents. The road to hell, Philip Roth once said, is paved with good intentions.

CHAPTER ONE

⊗

Ben was a teacher at St. Simon's, a private school for girls in Toronto. It was not something he had chosen to do. After two years in France he was living in a basement apartment on Heath Street, ten blocks from where he'd grown up, watching the girls from St. Simon's pass by his window in their knee socks and kilts. A friend, who taught there, called on Labour Day weekend and offered him a job. The art teacher had decided not to return after the summer. Ben had been building swimming pools for six months. Doing physical labour was exhausting. Why not teach part-time until he established himself as an artist? That was twenty years ago. Having no real ambition had left him stranded.

He looked at the new girl, Wanita Rosengarten, who had just returned from Italy a few days ago. It was the middle of October, about six weeks into the first term.

The students in this class were drawing a still-life arrangement he had set up earlier in the day. They'd been asked to draw as accurately as they could and to run the image out of the page on all four sides. A long piece of wood supporting four artificial pears, about eight inches apart, was placed perpendicular to the main grouping of elements. Wanita had chosen to draw two pears, blowing them up to fill the page. She had defined them with a light outline and was working on building form with a bold use of shadow and light.

"Nice drawing," Ben said.

"I can't draw," she said.

"You can," he said. "You have a fine sense of form."

"Look, I only took art because I figured I could catch up and get the credit."

"Did you take art at your other school?"

"When I was in Toronto my high school had a crappy art program and there wasn't much interest in the subject among my friends. In Italy there was art everywhere but it was not something I wanted to study."

"Where did you go to high school?"

"Forest Hill Collegiate."

"I went there."

"Did you take art?"

"No. They didn't offer it then."

"Where did you study?"

"Different places. Look, I can see that you have some natural ability and if you want to work you can develop it."

"Thanks. But my father is the artist in my family and one is too many."

"Why do you say that?"

"It's a long story."

"Does it have a title?"

"Yeah, *Father Knows Nothing.*"

"Mr. C, I need you."

It was Olive Chan calling from the other side of room.

"Keep working," he said to Wanita.

Olive spun a pencil around her knuckles like a helicopter blade and rocked her thighs together and apart, together and apart.

"I don't know what to do," she said.

"Just keep going."

"But I'm so bored."

He glanced up at the clock. He saw the minute hand move. It was the last period of the day. There were twenty-three minutes left. It was like watching water freeze.

CHAPTER TWO

He left the studio at four and went to pick up his son, Alexander, at daycare. Alex was eleven. Halfway there, Ben remembered there was a staff meeting after school. He decided not to go back. It was the fourth meeting since the beginning of term. The new Head was crazy for meetings and was sending a message to the faculty that the free ride was over and they would all have to begin performing like people with real jobs. Having a real job meant arriving early and staying late. The ease, autonomy and independence, with which Ben had spent his working days, were being shattered.

Alex was glad to see him and hugged him tightly.

"He hasn't smiled all day," his teacher said. "You must be good medicine."

Her name was Karen Oak. She was a sweet, nurturing, young woman from a small Ontario town who ran the daycare program.

"For you I would recommend an oral dosage three times a day."

"Only three," she said.

Lately, he found himself attracted to women like Karen. Women with a good sense of humour and uncomplicated goals.

He was forty-six and had been living with Gemma Kite for five years. Gemma was an actress, thirty-four years old, with a daughter, Franny, the same age as Alex.

He took Alex to the grocery store and bought three steaks for dinner. Gemma didn't eat meat. He bought her a piece of salmon instead. He shopped at the same store every day. It was around the corner from Alex's school. Usually he joked around with the butchers but today he wasn't in the mood. They were a humourless lot anyway. Good at dishing out the insults, bad at taking them. Theirs was still a tribal world. The family first. His was the opposite. His families kept coming apart at the seams.

Franny went to the Mabin School and they picked her up on their way home. She was the costume designer for the school play and often stayed until five or six to help with the sewing. Today she was preoccupied, worried about getting everything done, and reluctant to stop what she was doing.

Gemma's ex-husband paid her tuition. Neither Ben nor Gemma could afford the school on what they were making. They rented the top two floors of a house on Roxborough between Yonge Street and Avenue Road. The left turn onto Roxborough at rush hour was a difficult one. He had been hit once and the little Honda he was driving, totalled. He made the turn each day with trepidation and thought about moving.

CHAPTER THREE

At home Gemma was getting out of the shower. It was five-thirty on a Monday. Not a day she worked out. Why had she taken a shower? Tensions were on the increase with Gemma. He had been there before, been both the dog and the bone. Showers at odd hours were always a danger sign, like unfamiliar brands of cigarettes, or levity when there was no cause.

He watched her wrap a towel around her wet hair.

"How was your day?" she asked, turning from his gaze.

"Awful," he said. "The usual. I'm so bored I could cry. You?"

"Not much better," she said, stepping into an old cotton housedress and covering herself quickly. "I read for a film today. It turns out I went to school with the director."

"That's promising."

"I don't know. I wouldn't sleep with him then and I won't sleep with him now. He wanted to see my tits. I said no. It just felt like he wanted to see my tits. And now he's in a position to ask."

"That's not fair."

"What is?"

"I bought steaks and salmon for dinner."

"I'm going out," she said.

"Where?"

"With Charlie Kravius. It's a dinner with prospective investors for his play. I told you about it days ago."

"I must have forgot."

He went downstairs and started putting away the groceries. The kids were on the sofa watching *The Simpsons*. He decided to make them fries with their dinner as a special treat.

There were five potatoes but he only cut up four. One, with odd markings and a twisted form, he saved for drawing. He did one drawing from life a day. He had been doing this for many years. He approached each drawing as if it were his first. In a year he would only draw two or three potatoes. This one had a lot of nuance.

The kids laughed out loud and their laughter made him laugh, lighting him up for an instant. He thought about television and all the hours he had spent watching it since his family first got one in 1953. He wanted those hours back but they were lost forever. He opened a bottle of wine. He tore the lettuce and rinsed it.

Gemma came down dressed and ready to go. Teased hair, a black mini dress and no bra.

"You look hot," he said.

"Thanks."

"Show me your tits."

"Here in the kitchen?"

"Yeah."

"Later."

"Sure."

He pulled the cord on the salad spinner a few times and poured himself a glass of wine.

"How long 'til dinner, Dad?" Alex called from the living room.

"An hour, maybe. You have time to do your homework."

"Mom, where are you going?" Franny asked.

"Out to dinner, sweetie."

Franny ran over and put her arms around her mother's waist and rested her head against her breast.

"Mmm," she said. "You smell good."

"I gotta go," Gemma said, "my ride's here." She slipped out of Franny's grasp and kissed the top of her head.

"Bye," Franny said.

"See you later."

Ben finished dicing the potatoes and set the table, folding the napkins into triangles, giving them a festive flair. He drank a glass of wine, listened to some jazz on the radio, fried the potatoes and made a salad. He seared the steaks in a hot cast-iron pan and cooked them for about ten minutes, then called the kids to the table. They wanted ketchup for the fries and Franny got it from the fridge.

He had some quaint, old-fashioned ideas about dinnertime that were beginning to seem peculiar. As a family they sat down together every night. They might listen to music but they never ate and watched television. It was a time when they could all be together and for him it anchored the day, gave it a focus. It wasn't about love and the family and togetherness and communicating with one another. It was about the rhythm of the day. Some nights, like tonight, no one talked. They were hungry, preoccupied, tired. The meal had taken an hour to prepare and was over in twenty-five minutes. A glass of wine remained in the bottle and the kids both asked to be excused to do their homework.

They carried their plates to the kitchen and Ben spent half an hour cleaning up. He made an espresso and got out his drawing materials. The potato had lost its appeal and he chose an Italian pear from the fruit bowl instead. It had a long graceful neck and the stem was still intact. He stood it on the bottom of an inverted tumbler.

His drawings were done in 11" x 14" sketchbooks on all rag paper that had some tooth. The paper, natural and chemical free, would not yellow or disintegrate over time. This archival quality was important to him. Tonight he worked with pencils of varying softness, and though he had drawn a thousand pears each one required his utmost concentration and he gave himself over totally to the process. His mind, the cells of his mind, the molecules would regroup while he drew and the weight, the density, the blank fog that he was left with at the end of each working day would disappear.

If he wanted a career as an artist he would have to do more, produce more, take the drawings into some form that was more presentable, that had more gloss, that a consumer of art could relate to, because no one really paid attention to drawing any more. Poor, dowdy old drawing, the relative that time forgot, shuffling around the house like a widowed aunt.

A drawing like this, where he worked with short lines, building form and tone with cross-hatching, subtle, almost imperceptible cross-hatching, might take him two or three hours. He didn't mind. On a night like this what else was there to do.

He worked at the dining-room table, or the kitchen table, anywhere he was comfortable. He no longer needed a studio and all the obstacles to getting there that actually made working more difficult. When the coffee was finished he went back to the wine.

The stem of the pear presented the most difficult challenge. It was thin and delicate and this one was longer than most and curved in an elegant arc. He had to give it dimension, make it look round and strong, but fragile at the same time. It was the last thing by which the pear had clung to the tree, to nourishment and life. There were subtleties of light and texture that he couldn't see even with his glasses. It was less than a year since his last prescription. The rot never sleeps. He held the page up to the light. Squinting, he felt vulnerable and at the mercy of his age. Like the two or three times, recently, when he had almost fallen in the shower. He had closed his eyes to rinse his hair and leaned his head back only to feel its weight pulling him backward in a way that was beyond his control. It required an enormous effort, an act of will to right himself and stop the fall.

Alex came downstairs and sat beside him at the table.

"Nice pear," he said

"Thanks, son."

"Dad, I have to do a project for school. Can you tell me more about Alexander Calder?"

"He was no relation of course. But a great artist just the same. He invented the mobile and made sculpture move. He looked like a jolly generous man with a playful spirit. Not one of the gloomy, dark, depressed types . . ."

"Like you and your friends."

"Right. Anyway, on the bookshelf in my office there's a book with a red cover that says *Calder* on the spine. Have a look at that and we can talk some more."

"Okay. Do you think we could make a mobile?"

"Sure. We'll do it in the art studio one day after school. When do you need it?"

"In about two weeks."

"No problemo."

Alex went back upstairs and Ben put on a Stan Getz CD and continued with the drawing. Thoughts of Gemma caught him off guard and he lost his focus trying to push her out through the door she had entered. It worked for a moment then she was back. What was she doing? And with whom? Was she coming home tonight? When?

He opened a bottle of cold white wine and sat down in front of the TV to watch the news.

He was asleep in the chair when Gemma got home — an empty wineglass in his lap and a Polish film with French subtitles on the screen.

"It's a good thing you quit smoking," she said, bending over and kissing his cheek, "otherwise you would have burned down the house a hundred times."

She was right. And by the time he quit smoking a few years ago he only allowed himself to smoke standing up when he was alone at night.

She smelled of smoke and wine and the remnants of some cologne or perfume.

"Come up to bed," she said.

"How'd it go?"

"Fine. The investors were impressed."

"I'll be right up," he said, lingering on a scene from the movie. There was a naked woman, a girl really, and a boy watching her through a window. She squatted over a bucket and peed, the room lit only by the light of the moon and the stars. Ben peered into the TV then turned it off and poured a glass of wine. He drank it leaning against the counter in the kitchen. He was getting comfortable again with his loneliness and the reluctance to relinquish it. He chose the wine over Gemma who had invited him to bed.

But she stirred when he got there and moved against him, heat emanating from her arms and legs. He put his hand on her vagina and she moaned and threw a leg up over his hip. He rolled her onto her back and they fucked not bothering with any of the preliminaries, the foreplay that had become so routine. They kissed each other while they came, something that hadn't happened in a long time.

CHAPTER FOUR

꩜

In the morning he drove at a relaxed pace and did not get
angry when people cut him off, didn't signal, or decided to
brake in the middle of the road for no apparent reason. It
was the sex. It calmed him and was good for his complex-
ion. He dropped Franny off first and then Alex and then,
finding his own parking spot taken, he parked on the lawn
in front of the school. The Olds Cutlass convertible, black
with a black top, chrome bumpers and chrome wheel covers, that he had borrowed from his mother more than ten
years ago, looked like sculpture out on the lawn under the
plane trees. It was a 1968 and he had driven it as a teenager and every once in a while the 289 horsepower V8 would
give him a jolt and remind him of how out of control and
in danger he was as a youth.

He entered the school with his head bowed, his shoulders slightly rounded, trying not to be seen. The morning
chapel service was in progress and he was missing it again.
He had missed it every morning for years. But the new principal was aware of his absence and wanted him to attend.
She reminded him of his duty and his obligation to the
students and the staff, reminded him that he was part of a
community and must participate in that. Oh, he was a good

teacher, good enough, but there was lots left to be desired. He passed the front desk, pretending to be in a hurry, with no eye contact and a barely audible good morning for the woman stationed there. She was part of the new security arrangements. She went with the television monitors in the hallways, the hidden cameras, and the electronically locking doors. They were housing the children of millionaires, politicians, and Middle Eastern royalty. Security was a real concern. Soon the woman at the desk would be armed with an Uzi, no, not an Uzi, it was Israeli and the Arabs would not approve. Did Kolishnakov make a machine pistol? He would have to find out. Ben Calder, Head of Art and Armaments at St. Simon School.

In the staff room his mail box was full of the usual new directives and initiatives and invitations to sit on this committee or that, as well as all the many opportunities for professional development and growth that were tied in with gaining knowledge and expertise on the new laptop computers that were everywhere — breeding in corners in the darkness of the night, sending hundreds of miles on metallic conduits like tentacles along corridors and through walls.

There were only two people in the room, colleagues he had worked with for years. They were huddled together in a corner, head to head, sharing some new hurt or pain, some breach in decorum, inflicted or perpetrated by the new principal who came from the public school system and was not attuned to the culture, the rarefied customs of an independent school.

He went upstairs to the art studio to wait for his class. When they arrived he asked if any of them watched *Rocky and Bullwinkle*. One did. The rest just nodded, never heard of it.

"There is a thing they do on the show," he said, "called 'Fractured Fairy Tales.' Let's do Fractured Visual Clichés. Deconstruct the couple who are holding hands under the palm tree facing the low full moon and all the other images like that. Work on 16" x 20" paper with water resistant markers and either gouache or water colour. Any questions?"

"What's a cliché, sir?"

"What's wrong with that image? I was going to do it for my next painting."

"Does this count?"

"How can you mark art anyway?"

"Was your girlfriend in a movie called *Street Slut*?"

"Has she ever won an Academy award?"

"Do you like teaching?"

"I'd never be a teacher."

"School sucks."

"Develop your idea on newsprint," Ben interrupted. "I'll cut the paper for the final version."

The phone in the studio was flashing. There was a message waiting for him.

"Hello, this is Patricia Post. I noticed you weren't at the meeting yesterday. Please get back to me with an explanation."

He was forty-six years old and like a kid he was in trouble again. He replaced the receiver with a little more force than he had intended and knocked the phone off the wall.

"Good news?" asked one of the girls.

"The best," he said.

The students, in tenth grade, aged fifteen and sixteen, began work on their images. They sat on stools at eight-foot long tables. There were four tables in this studio and each could hold six kids comfortably, eight or ten if necessary. The more people at the table the smaller the work they could do. With this piece it didn't matter and Ben let the kids work wherever and with whomever they wanted while he paced around, distracted, trying to control his anger, preparing for yet another confrontation with Miss Post. She was the fifth Head he had worked for and part of the problem was his fault. She had arrived when he was tired, harbouring thoughts of change. He never bothered to pop his head into her office and say hello, how are you, how's the job going, blah blah blah, the niceties, the gestures of welcome.

After class he needed a document from the front office. To get there he would have to pass Miss Post's door. Normally he would just walk by quickly and not look in. He had been doing that for two years now. Today he felt like he had to respond to her call and he stopped in the hallway outside her office and tapped on the doorframe. She looked up from her laptop,

"Oh Mr. Calder, come in."

"Only for a moment, I have a class."

"This won't take long."

She stood up and offered him a seat on one of the two sofas in the room. He took a chair beside them. The sofas were too low.

"You weren't at the meeting last night." It was an accusation and a question.

"No. I went to pick up my son and I forgot."

"You forgot. You're a department head, a member of the management team and you forgot. You're going to have to perform better than that. You should think about stepping down if you can't."

"It's not like I miss that many meetings."

"Four last year and already two this year. That'll never do. And where is your feedback about the mission statement? It was supposed to be in last Friday."

"I want to give it more thought."

"Well, hurry up. And we have to talk more about the arts and a creativity-based curriculum. Book some time with Helgard for this week."

"Sure."

"Miss Surbiton told me you were going to be trouble and if you weren't such a good art teacher I'd fire you now."

He looked at her in silence, much like he had looked at his high-school principal, Mr. Lafroy, the morning he was expelled. Tyrants all, except for Miss Surbiton, who had a brain and had peered into the vulnerability of the human soul.

He got the updated class lists he needed from the office and went back upstairs. A student, holding the phone, waited for him by the studio door.

"It's a call for you," she said.

"Thanks," he said, taking the phone and wiping the receiver on his leg. So many young people, with a variety of viruses and colds used that phone.

The student caught him.

"I don't have germs," she said.

"I know. It's not about you. It's about the thousand other people who use this phone."

"You wanna sip of this?" she said, offering him an ice tea drink in a can.

"No thanks," he said, and spoke into the phone.

"Hi Ben, it's Karen. I hate to bother you at work but Alexander was in the daycare for a few moments this morning before classes started, and he was showing the same signs of sadness as yesterday. Is there anything I should know?"

"I don't think so, Karen. He has been a little quiet lately but seems fine at home. We worked on a project together last night."

"Has he said anything about school? Friends? Anything like that?"

"No. Could it just be a phase? Like when you first realize the hopelessness and futility of existence?"

"Yeah, it could be that. But I doubt it. I'll try to talk to him when he comes down after school."

"Thanks. I'll see you later."

He hung up the phone and turned to his class. They were putting finishing touches on the still life they drew yesterday, eating snacks and shooting the breeze.

"Girls, the model I booked for today had to cancel. I'm sorry. Give me a minute and I'll set up an arrangement of chairs and we can spend the class looking at negative space."

"We did that in Grade 11."

"Well, it's not like you do it once and you've mastered it."

"I'll model," said Alicia, a tall dark-haired beauty, whose family lived in Florida and the Caribbean. "I don't feel like drawing today."

"Okay," he said. "Everyone get a drawing board, a few sheets of cartridge paper, some soft pencils and come into the other studio."

It took five more minutes for the class to get ready to work.

On the drawing stage, beside the window, he draped a chair with canvas and Alicia sat down on it dressed in her uniform, her blazer off and her tie loosened at the neck. She sat parallel to the window, her legs crossed at the knee, one hand behind her head, and one in her lap. Her knee socks were down around her ankles and she wore boots with elastic sides, in protest against the required oxfords. The studio windows all faced north and the light was clear and consistent throughout the day.

"Okay," he said, "try and draw the model without using any lines. Block in the shadows as shapes, working from the darkest to the lightest. Don't be afraid to create strong contrasts. It'll feel weird at first but if you stay with the process your drawing will move to another level. You have a half-hour. Any questions."

"How much of her do we draw?"

"As much as you can fit on the page."

"I hate drawing. Can't we paint?"

"Shut up, Marla. Everything is not about you."

"Bitch."

"Girls, please."

He found some jazz on the radio, John Coltrane live in Paris, and the students settled into their work with the clarity of Coltrane's saxophone driving them, creating a unity of focus, of purpose, that would sometimes happen in an art class when the conditions were right.

He walked amongst the students to see the work they were doing. He looked at their drawings then up at the model. Once or twice, depending on the angle and the light, he was surprised by how beautiful Alicia Gardiner was and his eye would linger, for just an instant, on her cheek, her shoulder, her thigh.

Wanita Rosengarten had done today, with the model, what she did yesterday with the pears. She chose an aspect she wanted to draw, took a tight point of view and filled the page with that. Here, she worked on a three-quarter profile of Alicia with the head filling the entire picture space except for a little collar and tie and an inch of shoulder at the bottom of the drawing. It was solid and expressive work with a bold use of shadow and light.

"That's a fine drawing, Wanita," he said.

"That's a fine drawing, Wanita," someone mimicked behind his back.

"How come she gets all the attention?"

Girls, he thought. Some days it was like working in a minefield and he never knew what movement, what motion on his part would cause things to erupt. He had become adept at ignoring most of what he heard. It was easier that way. For all their self-centredness, adolescents expected to be ignored by adults and he thought they preferred it. There were ways of reaching out, of trying to get attention, but it was okay if no one responded, that made more sense, fit the self-image more comfortably. It kept the division of the generations in tact and nurtured the resentments and jealousies each had for the other.

"Thanks," Wanita said. "I've never drawn like this before and though I was skeptical at first, it makes sense."

"Alicia, stop moving your head," someone shouted.

"Sir, she keeps moving."

"She's doing the best she can for the money we pay her."

"Funny."

"How much do models get paid anyway?"

"We pay fifteen dollars an hour," Ben said.

"That doesn't seem like much."

"She just has to take her clothes off and be still. It's not that challenging. Where I came from people have sex for less than that?"

"Gross."

"Where do you come from?" Ben asked.

"Why, you planning a holiday?"

"No."

"Chile. Antofagasta on the Pacific coast."

"Never heard of it."

"It's a terrible place. Bleak. A mining economy."

"How did you end up there?"

"My father's an engineer. We move around."

Though he wanted the students to be drawing without distraction he was always getting caught in conversations like this. He couldn't help it.

"Okay, there are only fifteen minutes left," he said.

When her time was up, he thanked Alicia and asked if anyone else would like to model. Wanita said she would. She was tired of drawing for today.

"Can you stand for a while?" he asked.

"Sure. How?"

"Just strike a relaxed pose."

She did. Hand on hip, one leg straight, one bent with her toes pointing out. Head down, arm hanging at her side. Her clothes were ill fitting because they were all borrowed. Her uniform was on order. The black loafers were her own as were the black-and-white striped knee socks. There was something familiar about her, something in the way she moved and stood, something in the shape of her body, the proportions, the way it tugged at him.

CHAPTER FIVE

☙❧

Wanita held the pose and the students in the class worked and said little. She was a new girl and they weren't going to taunt her on her third day. The drawings they did were focused, sophisticated and on a much higher level than when he first started teaching.

"Thank you, Wanita," he said, standing near where she had been working. "You held that like a pro."

"I was in a magazine once," she said, coming over to pack up her stuff. "My father's friend, who we trusted, took some pictures of me and published them."

"What magazine?"

"*Zoom*. Do you know it?"

"Yes. And who was the photographer?"

"Lazlo Dresh."

Dresh was someone whose work most people considered pornographic. Ben liked it, though. Dresh had done a great deal in the last ten years to open up the parameters of photographic discourse.

"Dresh is great," he said. "I'd like to see the pictures some time."

"I don't think so," she said.

"How do you know Dresh?"

"He and my dad went to art school together. Do you have a portfolio I can buy?"

"Sure. I'll just add it to your art fee."

"We pay extra for this?"

"What we charge doesn't cover a tenth of the cost. See that 4' x 5' canvas over there. Eighty dollars. You might decide to do three paintings that size. The cadmium yellow, eighty dollars a jar. You pay eighty dollars a year."

"My parents are going to shit when they get the bill. Oh, that reminds me, my mom knows you. I was talking to her last night, telling her about my first full day of classes. She said you went to school together. Her name was Ellen Roberts."

Does the word boner mean anything to you, he thought, because that's what he got the first time he saw Ellen Roberts and it didn't subside for close to a year.

"I know your mom very well," he said, understanding now where the uncharacteristic and irrational tug came from when he watched Wanita settle into her pose. "I'll get you that portfolio."

He first saw Ellen water-skiing in a blue bikini, coming in toward the dock, at around eleven in the morning when he arrived at the cottage of a classmate for an all-day party celebrating the end of Grade 13. He was there with his girlfriend Rhona. There was something about Ellen that blinded him with an obsessive, crazy desire that caused him to chase her around most of that day, ignoring Rhona and everyone else.

He behaved badly and drank twenty-four beers between noon and midnight. Ellen thought he was a potential rapist and Rhona thought he was a prick, pure and simple. It was

their high-school graduation and the only time he got close
to Rhona all day was in the car on the way home. There were
two other couples in the car and Arty Claritz, the driver,
was the only person not to have had a drink at the party. It
was a good thing because around one in the morning they
got stopped for speeding and then taken to the little Vandorf
jailhouse for further questioning. Arty managed to talk his
way out of a ticket while Ben slept on Rhona's shoulder in
the back seat.

Ben called Ellen the next day to apologize for leaping
on her and trying to kiss her when it was clear she didn't
want to be leapt upon and kissed by him. To his surprise
she was friendly and agreed to go out for a walk later that
evening. They only lived a few blocks from each other and
walked over to a place called Hostos, on Eglinton, where
kids could smoke and drink espresso coffee and imagine
they were bohemians in Europe. Afterward, at home, in her
parents' den, Ellen let him kiss her and their kisses were
hot and passionate and spoke of reciprocal desire, but when
he put his hand under her shirt and tried to touch her
breasts she pulled his hand away and said no. Mentally he
could live with grounding out at first on the first pitch. It
was what had been going on for most of his life. There
were exceptions. Recently Rhona made a remarkable throw
from the wall to keep him from converting a triple into an
inside-the-park home run. They were naked on that play
and he had a condom ready to roll on, like a tarp to protect the infield from the rain.

With Ellen, the attraction was purely visual, his behaviour triggered by cues that he didn't really understand. In
his whole life there had only been one or two other women

he had desired as much as her. It was the way she moved, the way she owned her body. They were different kinds of people, with different interests. Ellen was really straight and he was already looking for alternatives. They danced around each other for almost a year. She didn't get angry or get tired of being chased and he kept making adjustments to his swing until he tried out for a newly formed league with girls who were serious about fucking while inventing a whole catalogue of games, more elaborate and destructive than baseball.

Wanita put all her work away in the new portfolio. It was only when she moved that Ben really saw her mother. Otherwise, Wanita was darker, shorter, and had a fuller figure than Ellen.

"You're limping," he said, as he showed her where the senior students kept their work.

"I broke my leg and it bothers me when it rains."

"It's not raining," he said.

"It will. Do we have art tomorrow?"

"No. Thursday."

"See you then."

"Yeah."

CHAPTER SIX

❧

At four-thirty, after checking his e-mail and clearing up some invoices on his desk, Ben went to get Alex at the daycare.

"Hi, Dad," Alex said, wrapping his arms around his father.

"Hi, son."

Karen came over to stand beside them.

"It's been a quiet afternoon, eh, Alex," she said, "except for Brent, who burped so loud during snack one of the twins blew the apple juice she was drinking right out her nose."

Alex smiled at the memory of that and then was solemn again, his smile like a match struck in darkness extinguished by the wind.

"Well, son, get your stuff and we'll blow this pop stand."

Alex let go and went to his cubby and Karen said, "I tried talking to him but he didn't have any answers. He said he felt fine."

"I'll give it a shot later on."

"Good."

"See you tomorrow," he said, taking Alex's backpack and heading for the door.

"Yeah. Hey, I saw Gemma in some really lame movie on TV last night."

"There've been a lot of those. Was she a coke-addicted nurse turned hooker?"

"Yeah."

"Great tattoo in that one."

"I didn't notice."

"Jesus and Judas, from *The Last Supper*, drawn across her back."

"You're making that up. I would have seen it."

"You can rent the video to make sure."

"You're teasing. I couldn't sit through it twice."

"I have to every night."

"Get out of here."

He and Alex stopped at the bakery on the way to the grocery store. He bought Alex a chocolate eclair with real whipped cream in the centre. Alex had never had such a thing before and he went into a trance of delight. When it was finished he asked if he could have another. Ben said sure. Some days he couldn't worry about the consequences of insignificant actions.

At the grocery store he bought veal scaloppini and rappini. He was running out of dinner ideas. Food that rhymed seemed to work. The butchers were no help. Today they were morose. Like they lost a bet or a relative died. He could handle their mood swings, what made it scary though, were the knives.

The eclairs acted on Alex like a truth serum. In the car he said he was worried about Ben and Gemma breaking up.

"You have reason to worry," Ben said.

With that Alex began to cry.

"I never thought you liked Gemma very much."

"I don't. But I like Franny. She's my sister."

What an idiot I am, Ben thought.

"Well, don't worry, we're not breaking up," he said.

"Look me right in the eye and say it," Alex demanded.

"I can't. I'm driving."

CHAPTER SEVEN

At home Gemma was sitting in the kitchen drinking coffee and reading a script. She had an audition tomorrow.

"Hi," he said, putting the groceries down on the counter.

"Hi, where's Franny?"

"Oh, she's still working on the costumes. I'll walk over and get her around six."

"Hi, Alex. How was your day?" she asked.

"Fine," he said, opening the fridge door. "Dad bought me a chocolate eclair."

"Mmm. Nice treat. I wish I had one of those."

"I thought you were off sweets. I would have bought you one," Ben said.

"I am. Just dreaming."

"I got shit again this morning."

"What for?"

"Missing a staff meeting. Big fuckin' deal. Last night they talked about uniform infractions and did a little more brainstorming about the mission statement. What bullshit."

"You should look for another job."

"I should. But what the fuck would I do?"

"Nice language," she said, looking over at Alex.

"Alex has heard a lot worse than that. And it's only words and it's how I feel."

"You don't fart in public when you feel like it."

"Not if I can help it."

"Well, you can hold the language in too. Just squeeze your lips together."

Alex was laughing at this.

"Fuck you. If I can't express myself in my own house where the fuck can I?"

"I don't know," she said, turning back to her script and taking a sip of coffee. She was avoiding his provocation.

He wanted a fight, a real yelling and screaming kind of brawl, the kind his parents used to have all the time, the kind he and Alex's mother would have in the cereal aisle at Loblaws, bringing the store to a halt, the kind Gemma always denied him, coming, as she did, from a more genteel background where people settled their differences with silence. He looked at the big picture window, with its view of the street, and wanted to throw a chair through it. He could see the glass smashing and anticipate the satisfaction of breaking it but he didn't. He just walked out of the room and out the door and cooled off in the fifteen minutes it took him to reach Franny's school.

The play was opening tomorrow and she was excited about the costumes and how they looked. At the first dress rehearsal, what had started out as bolts of cheap fabric from a discount textile store had been transformed by Franny and her team into articles that covered the actors with colour and brought texture to the drab stage.

"Don't forget you all have tickets for tomorrow," she announced, during dinner.

"Good," said Gemma, "I can't wait to see your costumes."

"Do I have to go?" Alex asked.

"Yes. We'll go as a family. Don't you want to see what Franny's been doing?" Ben said.

"No. Plays at school are boring. I don't go to mine. Why should I go to hers?"

"I'd like it if you came," said Franny.

"Too bad."

After dinner Ben drew the same pear as last night, concentrating on shadow and light, working with the edge of the pencil and his finger. It was the approach he had taught Wanita's class earlier in the day. Called *chiaroscuro* it was developed by Da Vinci who might have invented photography had he lived a little longer. Carravagio, Rembrandt, Vermeer, Edward Hopper, who else, he couldn't think, were the only painters to really master light. Elusive, fading light. The diminishing light of autumn. The autumn of his life. Trapped. Caged. Stuck inside of Mobile with the Memphis Blues again. He wanted to cry. Instead he allowed his imagination to guide his hand and the lower part of the pear turned into a naked female torso with a rich mound of pubic hair and long legs on skates, executing a graceful 180-degree turn. Arms, a pointy head and small breasts were added, and some lines etched into the ice to indicate movement. It was a bit of playful surrealism that he worked on for close to three hours. But he took no pleasure in the result seeing it as a betrayal of his vision, of the rigour and the regimen of his own self-disciplined approach.

"Nice drawing," Gemma said, passing behind him and looking over his shoulder.

"Thanks," he said, ripping it out of the sketchbook and tearing it into little pieces.

At eleven-thirty he opened a bottle of wine. It's what he drank since giving up beer. Six beers a night for years. Six beers on top of everything else he consumed. Around the age of forty he blew up. His face fat and puffy. He quit smoking and then he quit beer. He tried to do some exercise. The next challenge was to quit drinking all together. Red meat after that and french fries, then bread and cheese. He would pare himself down to nothing, get rid of all extraneous flesh.

He was often lonely and angry, and thrashed around in his existence like a spoiled child whose will had been thwarted by his parents, by some figure of authority. He wanted to be in control of his own affairs but wasn't. The five minutes he'd spent listening to his mother tell his aunt that she was leaving his father changed him. Something fundamental, something basic in the configuration of his personality, his vision, his personal mythology, his sense of family, love, loyalty, trust, dependency, safety, innocence, something was altered forever. He'd been a wild energetic kid with a crazy outgoing exuberance who was suddenly afraid. The fear lingered and became a constant anxiety. Drinking softened and blurred the edges of that anxiety. But he was no longer young and agile and there were con-sequences — the next morning weighted with despair, with cheap, common depression and despair, and all day there was darkness behind his eyes exerting a pressure like tears. He finished the bottle and prided himself on not opening another before heading up to bed.

And bed was just another source of discomfort, of silent unarticulated pain. This bed with Gemma's voluptuous enveloping warmth beside him. Gemma who needed sleep, whose livelihood depended on it, shook him off, thrashed and kicked, and swore she was asleep when he touched her. He took it as a rejection and most nights got into bed like a man trying to find a comfortable place to curl up between shards of broken glass. There was only one way to lie down and not get cut and, afraid to move after finding it, his mouth opened in a silent scream calling out for love.

CHAPTER EIGHT

He was teaching Grade Eight, his second class of the day, feeling the effects of the wine and too little sleep. The drawing assignment was a landscape from above, a small format piece to be rendered in coloured pencil. The group was having a hard time with the concept.

"Sir how do you draw a cow from above, a car, a kid throwing a ball?"

"Is this how a tree looks?"

"Can I draw the side of a house?"

"These mountains look weird."

"Can I be finished?"

"I hate this project."

"Can I go to the bathroom?"

"My mom said I can get a lip job for my birthday."

"Can we listen to the radio?"

"There are no black-coloured pencils."

He was standing beside Annie Highgate, helping her draw a pickup truck from above, when his mother, Helen, walked into the studio.

"Oh, those stairs," she said. "I don't know how you do it every day. Can they not put in an elevator or something?"

She was dressed in black. Black cape, black pants, black boots, black hair and black sunglasses. She was sixty-five years old and still striking looking. She carried a shopping bag that said Morgans, a retail outlet of the Hudson's Bay Company that hadn't existed for forty years. It was full of file folders and a few framed photographs.

"Mom, what are you doing here?"

"I need you to look at something. It has to do with that bastard, Barry Silver, who stole all my money. I swear I could kill that man."

Until then most of the kids had kept working but Helen had a voice that could clean an oven, and her words got everyone's attention.

"Mom, can't it wait. I'm teaching now."

"Oh, you're always busy. You never have any time for me."

He was reluctant to leave the class unsupervised but he had no choice.

"Kids, this is my mother," he said, "and I need to talk to her, so could you please work quietly for a few minutes."

"Sure, Mr. C, no problemo."

He led his mother down a narrow corridor into a small bright room with a few computers, some reference books and a number of white drafting tables. It was also a gallery of student artwork. As soon as they left the studio one of the kids turned on the radio. It was an old Madonna song, "Like a Virgin," and half the group started singing along.

"I got this letter," Helen said, "from my lawyer, this morning. They're offering me a ten-thousand-dollar settlement and to get it I have to waive all future actions that might ensue if some money happens to turn up in that family."

"Well, ten-thousand dollars is more than you were looking at six months ago."

"Ten-thousand dollars is shit. I'd rather stick needles into my eyes than take their lousy ten-thousand dollars."

"If you know that, what do you want from me?"

"I'm not sure. If I don't take it I may end up with nothing. If I do, I'll feel like shit for the rest of my life."

"What's worse?" he asked.

"They're both bad. My lawyer said I could hold out and maybe get more."

"Do that, then."

"It's a risk."

"Don't do it, then."

"Oh, you're no help. I have to sign this and get it back today. If your sister was here I would have asked her advice."

"Look Mom, it's a bad situation all around. You have to do what's going to make you feel less bad."

"It all makes me feel bad. I can't believe with all I did for that family they can just leave me broke like this. I hate that bastard and I'd like to see him dead. And his wife is no better. Five-hundred-thousand dollars they steal and offer me ten. And my stupid lawyer says I should take it."

It was then that Patricia Post walked into the room giving a personal tour to three Muslim women and their bodyguard. The women all wore tailored suits, stockings and high heels, but had their heads covered with a traditional black *hajib*.

"Mr. Calder, shouldn't you be teaching?"

"The class is at work. This is my mother, Helen Penny. Helen Penny, Patricia Post. Patricia is the Head of our school, our leader."

"How do you do?" said Helen, extending her hand, like it should be kissed.

"Fine, thank you," said Miss Post.

"Mr. Calder, these three young women are daughters of Sheik Amad ben Ibrim. They've come all the way from Barhouti to have a look at our school and they are particularly interested in art."

"Hello," Ben said, extending his hand to each of them. "If you'll excuse me I'll just check on my class. Have a look a round. All these framed works were done by students and they are good examples of what we do."

Helen did not make a move to go so Ben left her there with Miss Post, the three princesses, and their bodyguard.

His class had settled down with the principal's presence, and after answering a question about colour he went back to join his mother and her new friends. She was showing Miss Post a framed picture of Ben, taken when he was five.

"You were a cute child," Miss Post said to Ben when he returned.

"Thank you. In my family looks were everything."

"Oh, you never miss a chance to give me a dig, do you?" his mother said.

"What technique is that?" asked one of the princesses, pointing to a small print hanging on the wall.

"It's an etching," Ben said. "It's a good medium for teaching about planning and discipline in art. It's a little dangerous though and very messy and we can't get anyone to print on Thursday or Friday."

"Why is that?" asked the eldest princess.

"Because they don't want the boys to see them with dirty hands," Helen said, with a degree of impatience.

"Well, Mom, you should be going now," Ben said, putting his photograph in the Morgan's bag and taking his mother by the arm, he led her toward the door, with the others following, moving her through the studio, past the kids, whose work she suddenly developed an interest in seeing.

"Oh, that's lovely, dear," she said to Tasha Wilson, about her drawing of Camp Wantonobe in Algonquin Park.

"Thanks," said Tasha. "Mr. C doesn't like anything I do."

"Oh Tasha," he said, "I loved your self-portrait."

"That's true," she said.

"And what is the point of this drawing from above?" asked the youngest princess.

"Well, we're trying to get the students to think differently, to use their imagination, and not rely on cliché or images they've seen a million times on television or in magazines. This exercise forces each student to interpret a situation in their own way."

"Your culture favours the individual."

"It might look like that but there are enormous pressures to conform and they get worse with each passing day."

"How so?"

"Marketing, for example. It exerts a force on young people to be part of a group and not stand alone, and there are fewer choices with multinational corporations controlling the marketplace. Every store is filled with the same fleece pants and cotton T-shirts. It can be high-end like Banana Republic or low-end like Wal-Mart but it is all the same look made in the same Third World sweatshops."

"Thank you, Mr. Calder," Miss Post said, "but we really have to continue on our way. I'd like to see you in my office after school. Call Helgard and see what time is available."

"No problemo," he said, which got a chuckle out of Lenore Pendrath.

Miss Post led her group around him and he turned to see his mother engaged in conversation with Lauren Herwitz. Helen had a pencil in her hand and was helping Lauren with her drawing.

"Mom, you have to leave now."

"Lauren is Phyllis Berman's granddaughter. I taught her how to play bridge this summer, after Jerry had his stroke, and we needed a fourth."

"That's great Mom, now get out of here, please."

"Okay," she said, and gave Lauren a little kiss on the forehead. "Bye, dear, I'll tell your grandmother I saw you and how cute you looked in your uniform."

"I'll call you later," Ben said, as she reached the door.

"You know, what you do isn't so hard. I think I'll put my name in for supply teaching in Art."

"You do that," he said.

"She's right," said Annie Highgate.

"What do you do anyway?" asked Lenore Pendrath.

"It's a perfect job," said Liza di Carpo, "you get paid for standing around with a bunch of kids and doing nothing."

"Ain't I the lucky one," he said.

CHAPTER NINE

The class ended at eleven-thirty. He had to go to the bank and decided to have lunch in Forest Hill Village, a small cluster of stores, banks and restaurants, a block and a half from the school. It was two hours until his next class.

He had always seen teaching art as a subversive occupation. In the broader culture visual art had no value and meant nothing to the vast majority of people. By teaching people to make art, to talk about art, to visit a museum, or a gallery, to read about an artist or a movement, to buy art, he was helping to change that. But it was a losing battle and he felt like a creature on the verge of extinction whose thoughts and actions were at odds with his environment. In his way of thinking, his frame of reference, his artistic aspirations, and even his approach to teaching were in conflict with the vicious transition. He and a few others resisted the new management model with its emphasis on systems of accountability and efficiency and the increasing role of technology and were reminded, often, that what they did — teach art, drama, music, physical education, literature — was becoming irrelevant and obsolete; that in the current thinking about curriculum there was no time for these things and soon they would no longer be offered except as options to the few students who were not university bound, who were determined to stay out of the work force.

At the bank he needed to close three of his four accounts because the service charges were killing him but there was no one to help him, and it was suggested he make an appointment for the following week. He'd been banking at that branch since he was twelve and once knew the manager by name. The banks, growing extremely rich on the backs of their customers, had begun to feel such enormous guilt that they no longer wanted to see these customers face to face. They wanted them to do everything by phone or on-line.

He persisted and managed, with the help of a teller in training, to accomplish what he came to do. Afterward he went to a little Italian take-out with a few tables inside. Wanita Rosengarten was there at his favourite table, hiding out in his hiding place. It was a problem with the neighbourhood. The students were everywhere. He sat down at the table beside hers. She didn't look up. She was writing a letter.

He ordered soup, salad and a slice of pepperoni pizza. With the sound of his voice she stopped writing.

"Oh Mr. C, how long have you been sitting there?"

"Just a few minutes. I didn't want to disturb you."

"I'm writing a letter to my brothers, telling them what they're missing in Toronto, so they might put a little pressure on the parents to come home."

"Where are they again?"

"Near Greve. In Tuscany. A town called Montefioralle. It's really just a cluster of buildings. No stores or anything. We rent a house further up the mountain. Very isolated but a beautiful view of the countryside."

"How long were you there?"

"Over a year. I liked it but most of my friends are here. I was lonesome for people my age and I want to go to McGill next year."

"Are your grandparents still in the house on Vesta?"

"Yes. I stay with them on weekends. Papa isn't well and Mom thought it would be a real imposition for me to live with them full time. That's why I'm in boarding school."

The owner brought Ben's soup to the table.

Ben asked Wanita if she wanted something.

She spoke to the owner in perfect Italian and his demeanour changed to a light leering appreciation from the sombre deadpan of the burdened restauranteur.

"That was impressive," Ben said.

"I was the best in my family. The language just came to me. My father's hopeless and my mother caught on after a while. Now she talks like the locals and they love her in all the shops. She could be the mayor of Greve."

"Your mother had a certain, and I only know the French, *Je ne sais quoi*. Is there an Italian equivalent?"

"No. The Italians are much more direct. They would say she had a great ass and nice tits and she carried them with pride."

"That sounds about right," he said.

"She still looks great only my father doesn't see it. He'd rather chase young girls."

The owner came around the counter and presented Wanita with a bowl of spaghetti that had been tossed in hot oil and garlic.

"*Gracie,*" she said.

"*Prego.*"

Ben had some soup.

Wanita was more voluptuous than her mother had been and her face was already formed by experience. It wasn't one of the plump, well-fed faces of the kids in Forest Hill Village who park their parents' Navigators and Mercedes in front of a hydrant, in a no-parking zone, and go get a mochaccino while talking on their cellphones.

Though Ellen was probably the woman he'd been most attracted to she had been sheltered and lacked curiosity about the world. When they spent time together there were many occasions when he had nothing to say. One night he took her to a coffee house in Yorkville, the Half Beat, on Avenue Road. They went down by motorcycle. There was a folk singer there whose music and lyrics were raw and evocative, and Ben wanted to hang around and talk to him for a while, but Ellen didn't have any interest in that kind of person, so he took her home and went back to the club alone. He listened to another set and had a coffee with the singer. Ben was eighteen, looking for something different, a different set of values, a different way of life, and that put him increasingly out of step with the people around him.

Now he seemed to fit in fine; taught at an old established school and made little drawings that behaved themselves, raised his child and his girlfriend's child and talked to his parents and his sisters and managed to sustain a few friendships. But it was all like a prison to him and it had been since he started teaching. He was doing time and was not getting out earlier for good behaviour.

"My dad had sex with a girl the same age as me," Wanita said. "My dad's like in his forties. How could he do that?"

"I don't know," Ben said.

Oh, he had given it some thought. He taught girls after all but the body was such a small part of who they were.

"Would you like some of this salad?" he offered.

"Sure. And would you like to fuck me?" she asked.

He looked at her.

"Seeing you at a club or on the beach, or just walking down the street in a summer dress I might, but knowing you as your teacher and your mother's friend I wouldn't even think of it."

"Are you rejecting me?"

"Are you offering or asking?"

"Asking."

"Good."

"I'm trying to understand my father and you are the first man of a certain age I have been able to talk to."

"You want a coffee or something?" he offered.

"I'll have an espresso."

"You're simply too young and as a teacher my instincts are to protect you, to help you learn. I can see that you're attractive and there might be some pleasure in seeing the way the light falls across your skin, but the next step is not sex. Sex is so intimate, so mutual. There is so much distance to cross to get there."

"My dad's an artist. A sculptor. He's visual and sensitive. This girl he had sex with was pretty, but not that pretty. When I met her, people were lined up to be near her. It was some inexplicable quality. Even I felt it."

"Where did you meet her?"

"In Siena."

"And who was she?"

"She was some girl who modelled for a friend of his. When Dad first saw her she was naked in the studio. I think he fell in love with her but he couldn't admit that for a long time. He left me and Mom and the boys to go and be with her in Venice."

"Love changes everything. Love can't be traced or tracked down or pinned to the specimen box to be examined like desire. I can't tell you anything about love."

"He didn't love her at first. First they just had sex."

"Did he tell you that?"

"Yes."

"Well, we can't know the forces that were pulling them together."

"What if he was just horny and a little drunk and the moon was full and it was late at night and they were alone in a fragrant garden far from home?"

"That might do it."

"What about some self-control, some acknowledgement of the age that separated them?"

"There are situations where it is hard to be rational. It seems with most people that passions rule."

"That still doesn't excuse his bad behaviour."

"No, it doesn't. It does not excuse any behaviour. It's the circumstance of being human. We have only evolved so far. We're at the point where we can see another way, a better way maybe, but few can achieve it."

"How come you're so smart?"

"I'm not. I just pay attention to my mistakes and there have been many of them."

"Thanks," she said, and leaned over and kissed him on the cheek.

"You're welcome," he said, the words catching in his throat.

There was her natural scent and her breast brushing his arm.

He paid the cheque and she waited for him outside. They walked back to school together, against the throng of students who had just gotten out for lunch.

CHAPTER TEN

He saw Miss Post at ten to four. It was not how he wanted to end his day. She was sitting behind her desk and motioned for him to sit down. He and Miss Post were the same age, came out of the same social era and the same kind of education. But their goals in life set them apart. She was a manager concerned with operating systems and saw these systems as more important than the people they organized. He started with the people and forgot about the system. She had decimated the faculty and caused real pain and lasting grief to some of his colleagues. She was ruthless and he could accept that behaviour for a reason. Here there was no reason except the establishment of power, the building of a new pecking order. The administrative team ruled and if you were not on the team you were nothing. People were scrambling for the vice-principal positions being handed out like candy apples on Halloween. All you had to do was a little tap dance in the foyer or betray the trust of a friend. At last count there must have been ten of them and they all had secretaries and new offices that were once music practice rooms or small and intimate classrooms. The lovely old library, with its bay window and cushioned seat had been given over to the IT people and chopped up into little cubicles. There was no aesthetic at work in the implementation of the new order.

"Your mother was not wearing a visitor's badge. She did not sign in. We can't allow people to just drop in and wander through the building. There are security issues."

"She's my mother. She was not here to plan a kidnapping or to steal a laptop. Who is watching the security film anyway, especially the footage of the Grade Nine corridor where the girls get dressed and undressed in front of their lockers? You might check it out. Some unscrupulous member of the team might sell the footage to an Internet porn site."

"I don't think that will happen. Our visitors were impressed with your program. They would like help setting one up in their school."

"It wouldn't be possible to have an atmosphere that nurtures the creativity of the individual in a regime governed by religious fanatics."

"It's not so bad there. Your ideas might be a little out of date."

"I don't think so. The women in that country, the citizens, are allowed to be educated, but then not allowed to work. They spend their life shopping. The men rule and the royal family rules everything. They were bandits once and now they are the richest country in the world. They fund terrorism and would like to see the Jews in Israel driven into the sea and drowned. They are not a regime we should be aligned with."

"That's your opinion. We are reaching out to make global alliances and the revenues these generate will help fund things the school needs but can't yet afford. Girls' schools here are notoriously under-funded and have a great deal of difficulty raising money from alumni. We are trying to change all that."

"I've noticed."

"There must be things you need in your department."

"Not much."

"Well, I'd like to see a plan for next year. I'd like it in writing. The plan should include three goals for your department. Three new initiatives. Then we will meet to see how close you came to achieving those goals."

"What kinds of things do you have in mind?"

"That's up to you. Things that will enhance the visibility of your program. All the arts here need more of a profile. Independent schools in the U.S. are really show-casing the arts to great results."

No one could take a breath in the building now without it being used as some kind of marketing tool. The students were beginning to see all their personal accomplishments, whether being on a winning team or having some solo victory in music, scholarship or sport, turned into a public spectacle and photographed, then put up on the Web site and published in the new glossy magazine being put out by the advancement — formerly known as development — department. Names and titles were changed daily, randomly and arbitrarily. It was quite Orwellian, a debasing of language and a reconfiguring of the history and traditions of the institution. Only the old guard was disoriented by the moves, moves that seemed calculated to keep its members on their toes and to change the culture.

"This emphasis on marketing makes me sick."

"You can either get with it or get out. This is the real world."

"Have you noticed how all our discussions end in one way or another with you telling me to get with it or get out? Where is the intellectual exchange, the respect for a colleague?"

"You have to earn that with me. All I see from you is resistance to change."

"I am not opposed to change. I just don't agree with some of the new initiatives."

"Tough."

"That's what you have to say?"

"That's it. As the Merry Pranksters used to say, 'You're either on the bus or you're off it.'"

Hearing her quote Ken Kesey was sacrilege.

"I want those goals on my desk by Monday," she said, and stood up to show him the door.

Zig Heil, Baby.

CHAPTER ELEVEN

At the daycare the kids were outside in the playground. Alex was sitting on a tire swing being pushed and spun by a couple of girls his age. He was holding on tightly, frightened but screaming with delight. The more he screamed the harder they pushed. He had his eyes closed.

Karen and Zdonna, another teacher, were standing together watching the children.

"Hi, Ben," Karen said.

"How are you?" he asked.

"On a beautiful day like today, who can complain."

"I could, but I won't. Alex looks a little more engaged today."

"Yeah. He's been fine."

"Good."

"Zdonna's engaged. Show him the ring."

Zdonna, pretty with dark hair in a ponytail and bangs, fresh out of community college, held out her hand so he could examine the ring. The diamond was enormous.

"Who are you marrying, the King of Siam?" he asked, and immediately felt like an old man living in a parallel universe.

"No," she said.

"She's marrying Marty Beckerman."

"I know his father. We were in the same high-school fraternity."

"I can't imagine you as a frat boy."

"It was the biggest mistake I ever made. I thought it might help me get girls."

"Did it?"

"No, being in a frat didn't change the fact that I was five-four in Grade Ten and didn't have a driver's licence."

"Zdonna won't be working too much after the wedding," Karen teased.

"That's not true," Zdonna said. "I love working with the children."

The girls stopped pushing the tire and when it slowed enough for him to get off Alex came over to where his father was standing and hugged him.

"Well, see you tomorrow. Congratulations, Zdonna."

"Dad, can we stop in the Village for a treat?" Alex asked.

"Sure."

At home he put away the few groceries he'd bought then went upstairs to lie down. Warm as it was he kicked off his shoes and rolled himself up in the duvet. It was there that Gemma found him when she got home.

She didn't bother unwrapping him, she just lay on top of the bundle and kissed the side of his head. He opened his eyes, feeling a little queasy coming out of deep sleep.

"I got the part," she said, "and I didn't have to fuck anyone or show my tits. I do in the movie but that's another story."

"That's great," he said. "So you won't have to go to New York to find work?"

"At least not for a while. Let's celebrate."

"Franny's play is tonight."

"Oh shit, I forgot. After?"

"Let's see how it goes. We can always do something tomorrow."

"Yeah."

"You could suck my cock, now."

"And how would that be a celebration?"

"It would be fun for me."

"You didn't just get a job."

"No. I almost lost one though."

She started to move, pushing up on her arms, to get away. "Don't go," he said, "just lie here. I like the feeling of your weight on me."

"Just for a minute. What time do we have to be at Mabin?"

"Seven."

"It's already after six," she said.

"I'll give Alex something to eat. He asked for Kraft dinner the other day. Tonight can be his lucky night," he said.

"We can eat later. Get something in the neighbourhood."

"Okay."

She moved to get up. He wrapped his arms around her and squeezed.

"Don't leave."

"Let go. You're hurting me."

"Bitch."

"Asshole."

She stood up and he rolled over on his stomach pulling the duvet over his head plunging himself into silence and darkness.

CHAPTER TWELVE

Friday, after school, Ben was in his office staring at the
computer screen, trying to invent some meaningful goals
to present to Miss Post on Monday. He'd been up late the
night before, drinking until three and finishing a drawing.
He was awash in self-loathing. At the best of times he didn't
even have a language for the kinds of goals she wanted and
he resented having to find one and engage in this process.
He felt any agreement with Miss Post was a capitulation
on his part, an acceptance, his buying-in to the strategic
plan. He had no interest in being a team player, a manager,
or in aspiring to the next level. He turned away from the
computer and took out a drawing pad. There was a small
russet apple he'd saved from lunch but he had no interest in
drawing it. Since beginning this project he'd produced over
five-thousand drawings, in sketchbooks, that were piled on a
shelf at home. It bothered him that nothing ever happened
with his art, that it was never seen or sold, but failure was a
role he had become comfortable with and he would be disoriented if he ever achieved any real success. It was like love.
A breakthrough would shatter the shell of his solitude.

"Hi," Wanita said, coming into the office.

"Hi," he said, closing the sketchbook.

"Let me see what you're doing."

"Some other time."

"That's not fair. You get to see what we do."

"That's because I'm the teacher."

She was wearing what most girls wore when out of uniform and that was next to nothing. A tight T-shirt, with tiny shoulder straps, that didn't reach the waistband of her jeans. Her breasts emphasized by the backpack she was carrying and the fact that she wasn't wearing a bra. She held a small jacket in her hand and, though it was October, wore sandals with bare feet that peeked out from under the wide flares of her bell-bottom jeans. It was the sixties but more form-fitting, more highly tuned. Neither her belly nor her nipples were pierced. Perhaps because she was a recent arrival from a small town in Italy.

"I'm just heading over to my grandparents' for the weekend and you seemed a little down in class today so I thought you might like a treat."

"Oh yeah? What did you have in mind?"

"Do you have the Internet on that?"

"Yes. Of course. We are dues-paying members of the Global Village."

"Good. Check out www.claudia'sroom.com. I gotta go. Oh, my mom's coming to town next weekend for my birthday. She said she'd like to see you. I'll be turning eighteen, maybe we can all go out for a drink."

"I think the drinking age here is nineteen. You can get married at sixteen without your parents' consent, and you can vote and have sex at eighteen with someone who is not a teenager, but you can't have a drink after or during any of those activities."

"That's logical."

"Ask your grandfather if he remembers me teaching him how to ride a motorcycle."

"Okay. Bye."

"Bye."

Thankful for a distraction he went to the Web site she mentioned.

Claudia's room, he immediately recognized, was a room in the St. Simon residence and Claudia was Kristen Straight, one of his senior students, a white Jamaican, with a rhythm to her speech that was always a surprise.

Kristen sat at her desk, in her school uniform, working on her homework. She took off her tie and unbuttoned the neck of her shirt. She got up to answer a knock at the door. A girl came into the room. Francesca Sophia Martinez Ruiz. She was from Mexico, originally, but was living in Grenada because of her mother's lingerie and swimsuit business. She was a raven-haired seventeen- or eighteen-year-old and had been at St. Simon's, like Kristen, for three years. Francesca indicated that she wanted to borrow some clothes and Kristen said okay. Francesca took off her shirt and her skirt. She wore a bra and a lace thong. She kept her knee socks on and tried three or four outfits before choosing one she liked. She left the room and Kristen came back to her desk. She took off her shirt and worked on her homework. She stood up and took off her skirt. She wore lovely underwear as well. She held up a sign she had been writing. "How'd you like to put your cocktail in my shaker." She took off her bra and her underwear and squatted down on her haunches, facing the camera.

Ben watched the show. His cocktail was stirring. Claudia stood up and walked toward the camera. She was a white blonde with many freckles and a dark curly mound of pubic hair. She sat down at her desk and continued with her homework.

He quit the site. Then went back. A note thanked him for being the hundred thousandth visitor that day. He wondered how long the site had been up and running and had no doubt that he should say something to the school administration, to Miss Post and her gang of vice-principals, but there was something inevitable about a Web cam beaming out of the residence and he appreciated the audacity of the girls who were doing it.

His feeling was, if you were going to give the students all this technology, if you were going to reshape the entire approach to their education and base it on technology, then they were going to find ways to incorporate the technology into their adolescent rebellion. And his response, when the word gets out, and the site is made public in the press and other mass media, will be like Miss Post's response to him: "Tough." Tough titty, Miss Liddy. Technology was just another tool and St. Simon's had shown a real paucity of thought in elevating this tool to some kind of panacea for all the shortcomings in education. From a marketing point of view, it was argued, the only way to compete with the other independent schools was to offer a technology-based curriculum where each of the five-hundred senior students would work on her own laptop. That a little lap dance got thrown into the mix could only be seen as a positive development in his estimation. Technology breeds conformity and those that break free deserve some support. He shut down his computer and locked it in a cupboard beside his desk. It was time to get Alex and Franny and go home for the weekend.

CHAPTER THIRTEEN

That night, after dinner, he drew a pomegranate. He cut it in half and placed the two pieces on a small porcelain platter. He stood one piece on its end and laid the other down, with the inside, the exposed side of each, facing him. He worked slowly with a 2B pencil, drinking wine and listening to the movie Gemma and the kids were watching. It starred Steven Segal and was about a cop whose wife and kid get blown away by the bad guys he is pursuing. He gets hurt too and takes a long time to recover. When he does there's more trouble than the bad guys could ever imagine. There was always something satisfying about the way Segal's movies went to extremes of violence and sadistic brutality. When he gets mad, watch out, he might tear out your eyeballs and stuff them down your throat. The kids loved it and Gemma had a few laughs herself.

When he was growing up, the pomegranate was always present during Rosh Hashanah, the Jewish New Year, a holiday that had recently passed without them paying any attention. As a child he would go to synagogue two days in a row with his father and then, ten days later, on Yom Kippur, the day of atonement, he would go at night and most of the next day. Yom Kippur was a day of fasting. Sometimes there would be a pomegranate in a bowl on the dining-room table and he would see it when he came home for a few hours in the afternoon, starving, leaving synagogue with a headache, repulsed by the smell of so much bad breath in one place. He could taste the crisp tang of the pulp that surrounded the seeds and the bitter taste of the seeds themselves. Religion had been a central element in his life. It was both a system of belief and also a community. He hated going to the synagogue but he had friends there and saw the same people year in and year out, and the older ones all mussed his hair and said nice things about his dad, and his dad always introduced him as the one who would say Kaddish, the mourner's prayer, for him when he died. My "*kaddish suger*," he would say with pride, confident his only son would do the right thing.

Ben didn't miss the religion at all but he missed that sense of community, of belonging to a group. He had little to do with his aunts and uncles and cousins, and he had few close friends. He had devoted much of his early life to his friends but now they were gone, the bonds strained, fraught with tension and mistrust. That he was lonely there was no doubt. He longed for the easy time, the random rollicking conversations that they used to have over lunch on a Sunday with good food and wine and no thought about being anywhere else.

The white membrane between the seeds was particularly challenging in this drawing. He could only achieve it by leaving the page untouched, requiring him to plan ahead — drawing and thinking. It was when he knew he could do both simultaneously that he began to imagine he might get good. There was also much nuance here, in the tonality, the seed pulp was almost transparent, but the seeds were solid as was the skin. The shapes were irregular but there was some feeling of pattern, like a beehive.

Everyone went to sleep and he continued working, finishing the drawing after one o'clock. As was his habit, he signed and dated it in the lower right-hand corner. The work pleased him. He poured a glass of wine and plugged in his laptop. On line he went to www.claudia'sroom.com. Kristen and two friends, Estelle Long and Misty Lau, sat on the floor eating chips from a bag, Ripples with onion and garlic, drinking cokes, listening to music and contemplating a Ouija board. Kristen was wearing a long-sleeved nightgown and the other two girls wore flannel pajamas, tops and bottoms, with wild floral patterns, buttoned up and tied tight. There were wrappers and packages from other kinds of junk food scattered around the floor. The computer beeped, it was one-thirty. Kristen got up and left the room. The other girls continued to eat chips and look around. Misty reached into the bag and her face registered some surprise. She brought out a soft rubber dildo, jet black, about eight inches long. She dropped it like it was alive and screeched into her hand. Estelle was shocked. Ben was certain they didn't know they were on camera. They both stood up and left the room. Estelle came back for her half-empty can of coke. Kristen returned shortly and saw the dildo on the floor beside the Ouija board. She picked it up and licked it like she was licking away the salt. She then unbuttoned her nightgown and let it fall to the floor. She held the dildo between her breasts then turned out the light. Only her computer screen lit the room. She brought the dildo toward the camera making it look extremely large until it blurred then she put it down, got into bed and appeared to be going to sleep. After an hour he was convinced she was asleep. He went to www.pussy.com for some cheap old-fashioned porn but the site held his attention for less than five minutes.

He turned off the computer, had a drink of water and went up to bed. Gemma stirred and moved toward him indicating she was still awake, eyes-closed-don't-say-anything-just-touch-me, and he stroked her back and her thighs and thought about claudia'sroom and Wanita and Ellen. There was a nuance to the way Ellen smelled that he could still conjure. He played with Gemma's labia and her clitoris and she touched his penis and his balls and when she came he got on top of her and they fucked until she came again and he ejaculated, going through the motions of sex, while his heart waited patiently for him to finish, in a chair across the room.

CHAPTER FOURTEEN

Both Alex and Franny had soccer on Saturday morning. Ben took them and stood alone watching them play. Gemma usually went along. They would get croissants and coffee at Patachou and spend a few hours together in the park. This morning Gemma had a meeting with the costume designer for her new movie.

Rosedale Park was a tree-lined clearing in the midst of a residential neighbourhood. It had a soccer field, a baseball diamond, a hockey rink, tennis courts and a playground. Its out-of-the-way location made it difficult to access and, being surrounded on three sides by people's backyards, added to the intimate feeling of the place.

The 1911 Grey Cup game was played on this exclusive field. The University of Toronto Blues beat the Toronto Argonauts 14-7. A few dozen Rosedale residents stood around shouting and clapping, taking pulls from a flask, watching the game that was written up the next day in the papers with everyone else in the city wishing that they too could witness such sport. There were many private clubs in those days and this was just another version. Recently, private clubs had begun making a comeback, along with gated communities, only the lines defining the membership were not so clear, as true exclusivity was hard to achieve when it was only money that defined a candidate's worthiness. There was great snobbism in this city that began to fade when every institution, every private school and club needed money to function and to grow. Now Jews, Chinese, Indians, Italians, Greeks and Blacks were in the ranks of the establishment. Not many with real influence and there couldn't be a clearer picture of that than the Saturday morning scene at Rosedale Park. Ninety-nine percent WASP, the women in madras culottes and gum boots taking a break from raking the leaves, the men in clothes inappropriate for the weather, sleeveless vests, nursing hangovers, boyish haircuts uncombed. These people had something Ben would never have though, and that was a sense of entitlement. They belonged there, this was their park, their legacy and, though they didn't articulate that idea, it was something they'd all known since birth. Ben had roots in Toronto that went back over a hundred years, but it didn't matter because he was a Jew, and as a Jew he knew that in this place he will never truly belong, never sit back and feel completely at ease, never take the future for granted, never not think about the awful, brutal and unstable past.

Alex and Franny, in age, were less than a full year apart and so played soccer at the same level but not on the same team. Today, as happened about three times a season, they were playing against each other. Alex exhausted himself charging up and down the field, handling the ball, looking for, but rarely finding, someone to pass to and the coach, wanting to give him a rest but having no subs, put Alex in goal for the last ten minutes of the game. It was 1-1. Ben was anxious whenever Alex was in goal, especially in a close game, because he didn't want to see him let in the winning goal. He worried about Alex's feelings being hurt but Alex had something of his mother's laisez faire attitude in situations like this, and could take a loss in stride. He'd just laugh it off. He was competitive and worked hard to be a good player, but losing or making a mistake didn't get him down. In this way he was different than his father. So when Franny, on a breakaway, made a nice deke and scored the winning goal with less than a minute to play, there was no tension between the kids, just some teasing about the superior speed, grace, and skill of girls and, by the time they settled into lunch — chicken fingers, fries and chocolate shakes, at the Avenue Café — the game was almost, but not quite, forgotten.

"I know that move," Alex said. "Dad taught us both. I decided to be a nice brother and let you score."

"Did not."

"Did so."

Catching sight of Alex in the big mirror at the end of the room, at an angle he'd rarely seen, Ben was reminded of Alex's mother, Astrid, who was living in England and had not written or phoned in over a year.

A friend of theirs, from the old days, came into the restaurant just then and walked over to the table to say hello. Had Ben seen the friend first and thought about Astrid or had thinking about her conjured this particular friend she'd been fucking before she left?

"Ben, how's it going?"

"Good. You?"

"One paints a little, one writes a little . . ."

"I've seen your work around. It's everywhere these days."

"Yeah, I can't complain. And you?"

"Good. I'm working on a long-term project. One day I'll go public with it."

"Still teaching?"

The question like a knife between the ribs.

"Yeah. Kids, this is Norton Hammish. Norton, Franny and Alex."

"Wow. Alex, you sure have grown. It must be seven or eight years since I saw you last."

Alex looked puzzled.

"Norton was a friend of your mother's," Ben said.

"Oh."

"Any kids?" Ben asked.

"Twin girls. They're three. Let's get together sometime. Have a barbecue."

"Sure. I'll call you."

"Take care. Nice to meet you, kids. Oh, I've got a show opening at Moira's next week. Why don't you come by? Astrid will be there."

"She's coming to town?"

"She already came."

"She's here?"

"As far as I know."

Ben looked at Alex who put down the fork full of food he was about to ingest.

"Where's she staying?"

"I'm not sure," Norton said.

Some people fucked you every time you turned around and Norton Hammish was one of those people.

"What kind of name is Norton?" asked Franny.

"I was born in 1955 and there was a television show called *The Honeymooners*. There was a character called Ed

Norton. My family wanted to name me after my grandfather and they needed an N name and didn't want to use Norman. So Norton Hammish. A good name for a painter, don't you think?"

"It's okay," she said.

"Can we go?" Alex asked.

"I'll get the cheque."

CHAPTER FIFTEEN

Monday morning he was hung over. He hated starting a week this way but some nights drinking was good and everything else was bad, and those nights drinking got better and in time nothing else mattered. Astrid was in town and she hadn't called Alex. Alex was upset and Norton Hammish had rubbed Ben's nose in the failure of his marriage and his failure as an artist.

Kristen Straight was in his first class and they were working on a still-life composition begun last week that was taking longer than he had anticipated. The drawings were good though, and Kristin's was particularly good, and as she sat in her uniform, her shirt buttoned to the neck, the starched creases immaculate, her tie crisply knotted, he flashed on some of the ways she'd appeared on her Web site over the weekend. At one point, on Sunday night, she took a break from studying and put a black dildo into every orifice of her body, including her ears, and, with those floppy pieces of rubber sticking out of her anus, her vagina, her mouth, and her ears, she did a dance in her room, an erratic improvised ballet that would have made Martha Graham and the early twentieth-century *avant garde* proud. It was a scene out of Dali with rhythm. The more he watched, the more he began to think that there was a creative dimension to her site, a performance-art dimension that was about much more than exhibitionism. She was patient and brought real pace to the day and was totally natural and at ease doing whatever she did. Mostly it was the mundane, day-to-day things like work, sleep, hanging with friends, but then there would be these explosions of creative and erotic behaviour, some lewd and some just plain fun. If he was marking the site she would be getting 90's. Like her drawing, a solid, focused and mature work. She crossed and uncrossed her legs as he walked by. She was wearing stockings and patent leather loafers. He remembered that her family's business was communications, radio and TV, and for her to broadcast in this new medium made perfect sense.

The phone rang. A student answered it and said it was for him. It was the front desk. The model he had booked for the next two classes was here. He'd forgotten and sent someone down to show her up. He had used this model before. Her name was Sharon Gold and she knew her way to the studio but the new security policy required that she not wander around alone.

"Sorry about last week," she said, "but something came up and I had to go out to the airport and I forgot to phone."

"That's alright," he said, "I took your place and the kids were happy to see me naked."

"Yeah, right," someone coughed, covering her mouth with her hand.

"Could there be a more terrifying sight?" someone else said.

Sharon Gold was in her mid- to late thirties, a graduate of University College with an honour's degree in English, and she worked as a life model and a cashier at the Dominion Store in the Towne Mall. She went into his office to change while he finished his class and organized the east studio for life drawing, making sure tables and easels faced the stage. He brought out papers, pencils, conté and charcoal. After, he talked to Sharon in the office. She wore a red silk kimono with a dragon motif embroidered in gold thread and all her clothes were piled neatly on a chair. He once dated a girl who made a neat pile of her clothes, on the floor, before getting into bed. She was long, languorous and pale and did not say a word all night. The last time he saw her was the day Elvis Presley died. A night with Sharon, he sensed, would not be one couched in silence.

The class arrived, and when everyone found a place to work the session began. Sharon stepped onto the stage and took off her robe, striking a series of one-minute poses. Though her body was beginning to shows signs of age, the north light accentuated her voluptuous form while softening and blurring any blemishes. She brought a sense of drama and classical form to her poses.

Wanita was in the class, uncomfortable in her new uniform. She raised her hand.

"Sir," she said, "I don't know what to do. What's a gesture drawing?"

"It's minimal. You only have a minute and the idea is to capture the essence of the pose using as few lines as possible. Forget about detail."

Sharon changed poses while he talked. Sheets of newsprint rustled and were flipped over the drawing boards.

Wanita tried the next pose and had some success with the drawing. The one that followed was even better.

The one-minute gesture drawings were warm-up exercises to be followed by longer, more demanding drawings. First, a series of five-minute poses where a little modelling of form and a little detail was expected, as well as proportion and a fluid line. Then a thirty-five-minute pose to finish up. He asked Sharon to sit in a chair for this, facing the class with her legs crossed loosely at the knee and her head tilted back toward the window. The students had to deal with the foreshortening of the legs, which was difficult. Tomorrow, when she returned, they would end with a reclining nude in the spirit of Goya or Manet.

He moved around looking at the drawings. The best had the figure confidently placed in the picture space, cropped at the edges on two or three sides, and dealt directly with what was there. The worst had a small scrunched up figure in the middle of a vast empty space. These students never came to see the work as something outside of themselves. They only saw it as an eternal struggle. With them, his comments and suggestions came back like a ball bouncing off a wall. Some people were naturally visually expressive, others were verbal, others physical, others used the written word. Most people, he was convinced, could be taught to draw well enough so they would never say about themselves, "I can't draw." That's what everyone said when art was mentioned. It would be nice to eliminate that obstacle from the discourse and get beyond the limitations of a fifth grade perspective.

The previous summer, using Gemma as a model, he ran a three-day drawing class for a few friends and their guests at a cottage on Lake of Bays. Some great work was done by people who'd never held a pencil before. It was there that he met Sam Keitzer. Keitzer had a beautiful drawing style that could have benefited from more practice, but, in his case, life intervened. Ben had been meaning to call him. Maybe it was the light on Sharon's breast and shoulder that made him think of a drawing Keitzer had done while all the children took turns dropping from a rope swing into the lake.

Wanita took off her blazer and her tie. She unbuttoned the neck of her shirt and rolled up her sleeves. She was working in charcoal using white chalk for highlights. She blended with her hand, totally focused, working from the model's collarbone down to mid-calf, eliminating the head and the feet.

After fifteen minutes no one talked and Sharon Gold never moved. There was a stillness in the room, a quiet, not silence, you could hear charcoal scratching the page, and paper rustling, erasers, smudgers, a hand whisking eraser filings off the image, off the drawing board, deep breaths taken, charcoal dust blown into the air. He looked at Sharon. She must have sensed it. Her nipples hardened. The phone in the other studio rang. He went to answer it. The fluorescent lights were on, harsh and cold, an assault on the eyes so unlike the easy undulations of natural light and shadow in the drawing studio.

"Hello," he said, "Art Room."

"Ben. It's Patricia Post. Now Ben, what is going on? Just what do you think you are doing? Ben. I mean, who in the hell do you think you are? I asked you to have your response to the vision statement and your goals on my desk before nine this morning. Did you think I was kidding? I wasn't kidding. I hope you have them done, Ben. Because if you haven't, you are just showing me another way that you are not up to the job. Do you hear what I'm saying, Ben?"

He held the phone away from his ear and looked at it.

"I'm sorry, I didn't get a chance to do that over the weekend."

"You what? I can't believe this, Ben. I can't believe you would defy me in this way. Your time here is limited, mister, that's for sure. I'll see you in my office after school."

"I can't make it then. I have a meeting with Penelope Lionell and her mother. It's been arranged for about two weeks now. It's about her portfolio for Pratt and what she still needs to do."

"Then I'll see you now."

"I have a class now and there is a model here who I am paying. Next period as well."

"Lunch time then, 12:40 sharp. Don't be late."

He hung up. Working for her made him feel as if his existence was diminished, as if the world he inhabited was made small.

It was 11:15 a.m. He returned to the drawing studio. His class was almost over. Neither the students nor Sharon had moved.

"Five minutes, girls. Sharon, you take a break and we'll do it again."

Wanita's arms, her sleeves, the body of her new white shirt and her skirt were black with charcoal powder.

"What do you think?" she asked.

It was a stunning drawing. It took his breath away.

"Amazing work," he said.

"Really, do you like it?"

"I think it's great."

"Can I stay for the next class? Miss English? I'm just getting into it."

"I can't say yes. Ask your teacher. If it's okay with her you can come back."

"What about me?" Shawna Singh asked.

"You too."

Sharon walked over to where he stood, without bothering to put on her robe. She looked at everyone's drawing on the way. It was something she often did. She had a sense of herself, of how she looked, and she measured the drawings against that.

"This drawing is fabulous," she said to Wanita.

"Thanks."

Wanita left her drawing board and her materials and went to speak to her English teacher about missing the next class. The other students put their work away. Ben and Sharon talked. Students in the next class arrived before the current ones had finished cleaning up. Ben asked each to get set up for life drawing. Ben's colleague, Amanda Ketteridge, came into the room. She had used Sharon as a model before and wanted to say hello. Amanda had a printmaking class scheduled in the other studio.

The atmosphere was relaxed yet purposeful and Sharon standing naked, in the midst of everyone, only added dimension to the scene. The students coming in hardly paid attention to her. So it was apparent, from the moment she hit the landing, that Miss Post had arrived on the third floor, redfaced from taking the stairs two at a time or just enraged, it didn't matter. When she spoke, the room froze with tension and Ben could swear he smelled something vile and was reminded of a scene in the movie *The Exorcist* when little

Regan, possessed by the devil, turned her head around and her icy breath condensed when she said, in a hideous rasping leering tone, to the priest, "Your mother sucks cocks in hell."

"Do you hear me, Mr. Calder?"

He heard her.

"Outside, now, mister."

She was standing in the doorway of the studio. Arms folded across her chest, tapping her foot.

Wanita could hardly squeeze by.

"Miss Dack says it's okay, I can stay."

"Excuse me, young lady. What is going on here?"

"I was really getting into my drawing, so I asked my English teacher if I could miss her class to continue and she said it was okay."

"Do you make a habit of this, Mr. Calder, encouraging students to miss their other classes to take yours?"

"Only when it is appropriate."

"Outside, now."

"Sharon, start with five gesture drawings and a five-minute study."

It was only then that Miss Post's attention fell on the naked woman in the room.

"And who is this? Just what is going on here? What the hell is going on?"

"This is the model I told you about on the phone. This is a senior life-drawing class."

The students in the room were becoming agitated. They were trying to stay calm and pretend nothing out of the ordinary was happening, but it was not possible.

He took his time walking out of the room following Miss Post onto the landing. When he got there he thought she was going to hit him. Her hands were tight fists at her side.

"It is I, not you, who makes the rules around here," she said. "When I call you and want to see you, that is all that matters. I don't care if you're meeting with Mrs. Lionell or if you're meeting with the goddamned Bishop. I have a busy schedule, much busier than yours, mister. I start at seven a.m. and I go right through dinner. You don't know the meaning of work but you're going to learn, believe me."

He looked at her. She was shaking. It was Miss Wriggley all over again. His Grade Five teacher who used to keep him in after school and pound him against her bony body until she came. Miss Post was not bony and she kept her hands to herself but there was something unnatural about her hostility toward Ben.

"Do you understand?" she was saying.

"I'm sorry," he said, "I wasn't listening."

"That does it. I can't believe this," she said, her demeanour changing completely, her face bursting into some kind of patronizing smile, like she had been talking to an idiot all along.

"Twelve-forty then. My office."

"Right."

And she walked away from him, her hands behind her back, not exactly gleeful, but tilted to one side, a little girl who had just outdone everyone at double-dutch.

In the studio his students worked in silence. He didn't know what to do. What recourse did the worker have against a crazy and abusive boss. It wasn't the *Caine Mutiny*. It was his life, and his paycheque sustained his family and himself and he had no savings, no plans for another job.

Sharon stood for a long pose, leaning against the wall with her outstretched arms crossed at the wrist, like they were bound, her ankles crossed as well, her head tilted back dramatically, and her eyes focused on the heavens above. It was a pose reminiscent of Ingres, from a painting of his that had been cropped and used as the cover illustration for a recent novel. It was to be a thirty-minute pose. Ben walked around the room and looked at the work his students were doing.

Wanita was a shade darker and little channels of perspiration ran along the creases of her skin, glistening, like pearls.

She was oblivious and worked seeing nothing but the model and her drawing. In only a few weeks she had changed in a radical and fundamental way. She'd come with this innate talent, this drive to make something, and she didn't even know it existed until she got into this class. An opportunity presented itself to her and she embraced it, knowing intuitively it was exactly what she needed. He'd seen this happen a few times before, but usually in a more gradual way. Had she not come back to Toronto and come to St. Simon's this would not have happened.

"Hey, what's up with Miss Post?" asked Jane Jansen.

"What do you mean?" he said.

"Like she be the biggest bitch this side of Miss Marconi."

"I can't get into this with you, Jane," he said, wanting to really get into it. Miss Marconi was the head of residence and a ruthless opportunist clawing her way to the top of the administrative pecking order.

"They are both nice people who, like everyone else, have good days and bad," he said.

"Yeah, right."

"Sir, how long have you been at this school anyway?"

"Too long."

"Why don't you leave then?"

"I can't seem to get enough credits to graduate."

Sharon held the pose and he thought about fucking her to ease the tensions of the day. Then he thought about fucking her on the stage in front of the class. That might get some of the less involved students to pay attention.

There was a teacher he had read about once, who came into the classroom and sat down at his desk and said to his students that he was going to show them something they had never seen before. He then took out a handgun and shot himself in the head.

Sharon hung around after the class in no real hurry to leave or to get dressed. They sat in the office and talked for a while. There was water on the roof outside the window and he watched the ripples of reflected sunlight tremble on Sharon's body.

"I've been doing some writing," she said.

"How's it going?"

"Terrible. I don't have any feel for fiction."

"Write something else then. Poetry or journalism. How about a memoir?"

"Yeah. I work as a cashier at Dominion and I fucked a hundred guys. The first was Bob when I was seventeen. I fucked him on a train."

"Sounds good to me."

"It would. Men are all the same."

"Really. There is an interesting story in a woman like you. Bright, well educated, who has chosen to live the life you do. You just have to find a style or a voice for the telling."

"You think so?" she said.

"Yeah," he said, always the teacher — wishing he wasn't — tired of listening to girls, and women like Sharon, without a real direction in life, in their late thirties, without a child and with a body in decline, who came at you tits forward, as a challenge almost. Sharon crossed and uncrossed her legs. She had a gold stud in her labium. He could have sex with her right there and he wanted to have sex with her, he could feel himself stirring, it was the lack of obstacles and the clarity of the message but he knew that he had little to say to her and when it was over, as it inevitably would be, he would have to shut the door on any further interaction and he just didn't have the heart to do that any more.

Amanda Ketteridge came into the office then. Her class had run late.

"Sharon, I was wondering if you would be available next Thursday between ten and twelve-thirty," she said.

"Let me look."

Still undressed, Sharon bent over to find her day-timer in the big handbag she carried.

"That looks good," she said.

"I was thinking we could do something with costumes," Amanda said. "Have you got some flowing layered thing that will catch the light and create dimension?"

"I think so. If I don't, I'll make it up with a bunch of silk and chiffon scarves."

"Sounds good. I'm going for lunch. Sharon, do you want lunch? It's on us."

She looked over at Ben who gave her no indication of his thoughts.

"Sure, that would be nice," she said.

"I'll come down in few minutes," Ben said, "I've got a few things to do."

There was a knock at the door.

"Come in."

It was Wanita.

Sharon was standing in the middle of the room putting on her underpants.

"Mr. Calder, I was wondering if you had time to look at my drawing."

"Sure," Ben said. "Thanks, Sharon. If I don't make it down to the lunchroom I'll see you tomorrow."

CHAPTER SIXTEEN

⊙⊙

At home he looked at the things on his desk, the work he was supposed to do, and had a beer instead. It was five-thirty and Gemma was at a rehearsal. The kids were on the sofa watching TV. He took his sketchbook and started to draw them. First Franny and then Alex. Wanita's drawing this morning made him want to draw people again. The kids ignored him and watched their shows. He knew he couldn't do what Miss Post was asking. It was pointless and he was beyond spending his time doing pointless things for other people. There was a lot of Franny's father in her face, and in Alex a real presence of his mother, Astrid. Astrid took Ben's breath away and when she left he was weak with the loss for months and months. Drawing the children always made him think about the past. He finished and gave the kids dinner then walked over to Yonge Street to get some Phad Thai to go. He bought an extra order in case Gemma came home hungry.

He ate slowly and drank a few more beers. Gemma called to say she wouldn't be home until at least midnight. He put her noodles in the fridge.

The kids went to bed at ten and he took a spin on the World Wide Web, landing eventually at claudia'sroom.com.

It was quiet in the room and the lights were low. A girl he recognized, whose name he didn't know, was sitting in a chair talking directly to the camera. She was dressed in a baggy sweatshirt and jeans. The sleeves of the shirt pulled right down and cupped in her hands. Her face kept moving in and out of the light.

"I hated thinking about food," she said. "Every day all I thought about was food. What I was eating, what I was not. I didn't want to eat anything but it was hard. I couldn't keep saying to my mother at dinner time that I wasn't hungry. So I started to eat, deciding it was easier to eat and then throw up. Throwing up is gross though. The little bits of food get stuck in your throat and your sinuses. So when you blow your nose pieces of food come out. It's awful and it smells bad and sometimes when I first started the barf would splash back on my shirt and then I would have to change. I learned to take off my shirt before throwing up. I know that it is bad for my teeth, they are getting yellow. Some days I'd have a sore throat. It would be so easy if you could just get the body you want. Like, if you could just order it up and have it for life. It's so hard worrying about your body and how it looks all the time."

She rubbed her hands together as she spoke, pulling on her fingers and her sleeves.

"When I first started cutting myself I did it as joke. We were waiting to get into a movie and I found a piece of broken glass and I, like, dragged it across my arm a bunch of times and didn't feel anything. I thought I was scratching myself, then when I stood up and the line started to move I looked down and saw there was a lot of blood. I washed it off in the bathroom and it stopped. The cuts weren't too deep. Now, though," and here she pulled up her sleeve showing deep ugly gashes in her arm, raw and painful, "I sometimes have to get stitches. I know I should stop the cutting. I don't even know why I do it."

He thought he was going to cry. Anorexia was becoming a big problem among the girls at school. There were a few skeletal ones he taught, who looked to be on the verge of death. They would spend time in hospital and then weeks later come back to class. He knew about bulimia and about cutting as well but he'd never seen the wounds nor listened to someone speak calmly about her condition.

"Thank you E," said Kristen, coming into the frame. "Tomorrow, N and G will speak about abusive parents. This has been another episode of *The Best Years of Our Life* and I'm Claudia saying goodnight."

A few stills, highlights from the site, flashed on the screen and then it all went dark. He turned off his computer. He didn't move for a long time.

CHAPTER SEVENTEEN

Ellen arrived from Italy on Thursday. After not speaking to each other for over twenty years, she and Ben talked briefly on the phone and made a plan to meet that involved drinks at her parents' house on Friday night, then out to a restaurant for dinner to celebrate Wanita's birthday. It was a good plan. The only catch was he had to get a babysitter. Gemma was rehearsing most nights. There was a girl, Cathy, who lived a few doors east on Roxborough but she was busy. Sometimes he used boarding students as sitters and put a call out in his classes to see if any one was interested. Miranda Kane, in Grade 12, would do it for seven dollars an hour instead of the usual five. He would have to pick her up and drop her off. Miranda was always in need of money even though her father was a doctor in Sault Ste. Marie. For Ben it was a question of which student would go through his drawers when the kids were asleep and which one wouldn't. Miranda was a little vague when it came to certain details and she had about her a small-town pothead quality. He figured she wouldn't be too interested in poking through his stuff.

Ellen's parents lived on Vesta Drive, north of Elderwood, in Forest Hill Village. Her father was recently confined to a wheelchair and under the constant care of a Philippino woman. Passing by the house, Ben had often seen him sitting out in the driveway, taking the sun, with the care-giver by his side. He wasn't sure if Ellen's mother was alive or not but when he arrived it was she who greeted him at the door. Still slender with long black hair, an elegant woman, with a lovely face that hid nothing of her age.

Mrs. Roberts called Ellen, and Ben stepped into the vestibule to wait for her. It still smelled the same, a mix of sunlight and dust. He had waited there often, as neither Mrs. nor Mr. Roberts ever invited him in until Ellen arrived at the door. They must have sensed his intentions toward their daughter were always bad. It had been more than twenty-five years since he last stood on that spot, a horny teenager, and when he saw Ellen now, barefoot, in an old pair of jeans and a T-shirt, it was like no time had passed between them. The years of nagging darkness, of falling and failure, the struggle, the weight, the pressure behind his eyes, it all lifted, like nothing had transpired in all those years. It was like some weird transcendent experience, her body untouched by age, the body he could still recognize, in a crowd of millions, as belonging only to her. Women liked to say that men had cocks for brains, but it was really about the eyes, about what the eyes see, about an individual's idiosyncratic obsessions, as personal as a fingerprint, the nuance of the seen form triggering desire. He hesitated when he saw her, finding it hard to speak until they hugged. She fit his body like she always had. Their bones meeting in the right places. They hugged for a long time. Wanita coughed discreetly at her mother's back. He was sure Mr. and Mrs. Roberts were thinking, "Oh no, here we go again," only when he took a good look at Mr. Roberts he wasn't certain if he was thinking anything at all.

"Hello," Ben said, walking over to shake the old man's hand. "Remember when I let you drive my motorcycle and you popped the clutch, doing a wheelie that just about dropped you on the ground?"

Mr. Roberts smiled but didn't say anything and his hands remained on his lap.

"Stroke," Ellen said. "He has his wits about him but he can't walk or speak. It's going to make the cottage a real ordeal."

Ben patted the old man's back in a gesture of affection.

"You look great," he said to Ellen.

"Thanks. You don't look so bad yourself. All those young girls must keep you busy."

"It's the three flights of stairs, not the girls. This one is a real talent though. She already knows more than I do. Happy birthday, Wanita."

"Don't I get a hug too?"

"Sure," he said, opening his arms

She came at him like she was trying to prove a point.

"I brought you something," he said, stepping out of her embrace, like a parent trying to get out the door, to catch a movie, without wanting to upset a clinging child.

"Thank you," she said, accepting the hastily wrapped package he produced from his jacket pocket.

"So, you're living in Italy," he said to Ellen.

"For the time being," she said.

"Mom!" Wanita said, with the impatience of one who has heard it before.

"Where?" he asked.

"Montefioralle. It's near Greve. In Tuscany. It's a beautiful village."

"I know it," he said. "We did a walking trip through that region. I was teaching printmaking in Siena."

"When was that?"

"About five years ago."

"Before our time."

"This is great," Wanita said, holding up a tin box with a set of drawing pencils ranging from 3H to 9B, and a small sketchbook. "Thanks," she said, and kissed him on the cheek.

"Well, let's have a toast to the birthday girl," Ellen said, "and then we can go and get something to eat. I made a reservation for eight o'clock at Brownes."

"Brownes?"

"Yes. You know it?"

"Sure. It's in my neighbourhood. I'm surprised at the choice. With you living in Italy and all."

"That's just it. Something a little different. Where do you live now?"

"On Roxborough, between Yonge and Avenue Road."

"Oh, for heaven's sake. We used to live on Cottingham at Avenue Road."

"What house?"

"Number 175. It's on the laneway on the south side."

"I love that house. I pass it every day when I take my daughter to Mabin."

"Wanita went to Mabin and so did her brothers."

"Wow. We could have been seeing each other every day."

"Instead of not seeing each other ever in all these years," she said. "I didn't know you had a daughter."

"My girlfriend's daughter, Franny. I've raised her since she was six. She and Alex are the same age. Eleven."

"Oh."

Brownes was a neighbourhood place serving Rosedale and Forest Hill Village. The room itself was comfortable and not fussy, bistro style with clean lines and no excess. It was popular and usually full of businessmen and upscale locals, men in suits, women who were a little arid. Ben didn't go there often, even though he liked the food. It was the ambience and the fact that, more often than not, he would see the parents of one of his students and have to engage in some uncomfortable small talk.

When they arrived, Ellen and Wanita were greeted by the owner like a couple of old friends and after catching up they were seated at a corner table on the far side of the restaurant. Ben sat beside Ellen on the banquette and Wanita sat on a chair, facing them, with her back to the room. At the last minute Mrs. Roberts had decided not to come with them.

The restaurant was packed, the noise level high. Ellen had changed out of her jeans into a simple black dress, stockings and heels. Wanita wore a red V-neck sweater, a jean skirt and low boots. Ben was in black and grey. Other than a few women, he had the longest hair in the room, which even now, after years of long hair, still made an impression on the four men, at the table beside them, who had to have some kind of cheap laugh at Ben's expense. It was that kind of place.

Wanita had champagne at the house and was now having her first glass of wine. She had flushed cheeks and various aspects of her bosom would appear in the V of her sweater depending how she leaned forward and what she did with her arms. She was animated and giddy, a little hyper maybe, and managed to hold the attention of both Ben and her mother, telling stories about school and the differences between Italy and Toronto.

Ben could feel Ellen beside him.

"I miss you so much," Ellen said to Wanita, as the waiter approached their table carrying the first course. "I miss having a girl around the house."

"Thanks, Mom, I miss you too. You should try boarding school some day. I'm surrounded by girls. Some nice, some really nasty."

"I'm sorry, honey. It was a compromise," Ellen said. "It would have been too much to ask Nanna and Poppa to take on the responsibility right now."

"I know that. That wasn't what I was saying."

Wanita and Ben were having salad and Ellen the grilled tiger shrimp on a bed of fresh fennel.

"How are your boys doing, you know, handling village life in a foreign country?" Ben asked.

"They're fine. It took a few months, the first year, for them to get enough Italian to be able to feel like they were fitting in at school and not just oddities in town. The fact that there are two of them helped. It is a little village and, except for one British couple, the people are rooted to the land. Vineyards, orchards, livestock, flowers. Not simple people, but not worried about much outside their own domain. My boys are pretty sturdy and can hold their own in sports, and they both laugh easily."

Now, she showed signs of missing the boys.

"How are the shrimp?" Ben asked.

"Delicious," she said in mid-bite. "And the Italians, they love children."

"How'd you end up in Italy, anyway?"

"My husband. He had a breakdown."

"Mom."

"One day he left and I decided to follow him. It was time for a change anyway. The possibilities on Cottingham Street were limited."

"Mom, you never thought about the possibilities. You were just happy with your life."

"My parents didn't call me Sarah Bernhardt for nothing."

Wanita didn't get the reference.

"A famous actress," Ben said, "at the turn of the century. Jewish."

"Ever the teacher," Ellen said.

"If I had to choose, you would have been the last person I'd have thought would move to Europe. You were so rooted here and so conventional."

"People change. Life is not static. Look at you. You were a wild man and now you're a teacher in an old WASP school. The heart of convention, of the establishment."

"I know. One failed marriage, one kid, a body of work that no one wants to see, one day leads to the next. It's pathetic, really."

"You make it sound so dreary," Wanita said. "But you're such a good teacher. Look at what you've done for me. In just a few weeks. And you're happy there, in the studio."

"Thanks, Wanita."

"Maybe that's all there is," Ellen said. "Teaching is your calling and you're good at it."

"I get nothing from being good at teaching. Being good is part of the job."

"What gives you satisfaction?"

"My drawing."

"Why?"

"It doesn't come easy and there is pleasure in making something where nothing existed before."

"That's what Dad says," Wanita said. "I remember the first day I was in Italy. Dad and I had lunch and then we were sitting on the terrace having a smoke and he started piling these rocks up in the grass. Then he had this goofy, satisfied look on his face. I said what's that and he said, art."

"You smoke? Your father let you?"

"You can make something that conforms to your vision, your decisions," Ben said. "You're like a God, totally in control of the process."

"But men do that with everything in their lives and frankly I'm sick of it. I'm sick of following men around. Sick of their whining and bellyaching. Men do what they want and women wait around until they are finished. How long have you been smoking?"

"That's not true anymore," Wanita said.

"Yes it is," said Ellen. "Even with the most successful and accomplished woman. If there's a man in her life, she defers to him."

"That hasn't been my experience," Ben said.

"Then you must give women nothing."

"That's possible."

"Mom. Don't you think that's a little cruel."

"It's okay, Wanita. She might be right."

"Or the women are totally liberated," Wanita said.

"Or crazy," Ben said.

The waiter arrived with their dinner then. Wanita was having the pizza with four cheeses, Ellen the lamb shanks, and Ben the steak frites. The waiter poured them each a partial glass of wine with what remained in the bottle and they ordered another.

"I've been smoking for about three years," Wanita said. "But I don't smoke much. At parties mostly. Sometimes when I study. Everyone smokes at school."

"You should quit now," Ellen said, "while it's still easy."

"Your mother's right," Ben said. "I quit five years ago and I've been in a bad mood ever since."

"Maybe that's why all the women leave you," Ellen said.

"They left when I was smoking."

"There you go."

"I started in junior high."

"Ben used to smoke, ride a motorcycle and he wanted to be an artist. He was very handsome as well. Not your typical Forest Hill boy. I had a huge crush on him and when he asked me out I thought I would die."

"So what happened?"

"Not much. We didn't have a lot in common. Except this real attraction for each other."

Ben saw her coming out of the corner of his eye. He wanted to hide but there was no place to go. It was Estella Jacobson's mother. Irene, he thought, but couldn't remember.

"You naughty man. You walked right past our table without saying hello."

"Gosh, I didn't even see you," he said, getting up to shake her hand.

"Ellen, Wanita, this is Mrs. Jacobson."

"You can call me Kate."

"Kate's daughter is in my class."

"How's she doing?"

"Oh great, you know, she's very talented."

"She loves art and she loves your class."

"That's good to hear. How's your dinner?"

"Good. I'm just here with a girlfriend. Micky's out of town. Well, I just wanted to say hi. Nice to meet you both."

"You too."

"Bye," Ben said, sitting down.

"See you next week," she said.

He looked at her with an expression of incomprehension.

"Parent's night," she said, turning to leave.

"Oh yeah, right."

"Maybe I should make an appointment," Ellen said.

"Sure," he said, "I could show you things few others get to see."

"Mr. Calder," Wanita said, "that's my mother."

"I would like to see Wanita's art work," Ellen said.

"Sunday afternoon?"

"I'll let you know. These women must come on to you all the time."

"Was that a come-on? I didn't notice."

"You must be blind or stupid."

"Well, I am a visual person."

"There you go."

He was detecting an edge with Ellen and he didn't know where it was coming from. Was it about her in the present or him and her in the past? The second bottle of wine softened everything though and, conforming to the contours of the banquette, they had dessert in a row of three, with Wanita leaning against his shoulder. It was after midnight when they go up from the table and they were the last ones to leave the restaurant.

Outside, he stumbled, caught his toe on a raised piece of concrete sidewalk. He didn't fall but his balance was impaired by the wine he had drunk. They flagged a cab and he left his car on Woodlawn. He'd pick it up tomorrow.

At the house he asked the driver to wait and walked them to the door. Wanita was a little tipsy and leaned heavily on his arm.

"How about a nightcap," Ellen offered, "once we put the birthday girl to bed."

"No Mom, I'm fine," she protested without much conviction, and headed straight for the stairs when the door was opened, her tongue finding its way into Ben's mouth when he leaned down to give her a goodnight peck on the cheek.

"Sure," he said. Startled by that kiss, "I'll pay the cab."

Ellen left the door opened and he waited for her at the foot of the stairs. The house was dark and quiet like when they used to come home from a date.

"That girl," she said, coming toward him, barefoot on the thick broadloom. "She's fast asleep, blissfully drunk. What can I get you? Wine, beer, cognac, grappa?"

"What do you feel like?"

"A glass of wine would be fine."

"Me too."

"Let's see what's in the cellar."

It was a room he had never been in. The door opening off the rec room was covered in the same padding as the walls, making it almost invisible. When he saw the wine cellar he knew why. Her father had a significant collection of wines. Some going back to the late Forties.

"Wow," he said.

"Yeah. It's too bad my Dad won't get to drink much more of this. It was something that gave him a lot of pleasure. Every night he'd have two glasses with dinner and toss the rest if there was no one around to finish it. My Mom rarely drank."

"Some of these wines are worth a fortune."

"You know wine?"

"Not really. I put a twenty-dollar max on what I buy and look longingly at the rest."

"Well, how about this?" she said, taking down a '79 Brunello di Montalcino. "It grows a few kilometres from where I live."

"Looks good to me."

In the kitchen, getting a corkscrew and two glasses, they tried to be quiet, almost whispering, and opened doors and cupboards with delicacy and caution. It was an experience he hadn't had in a long time — being in someone else's place late at night, moving from one patch of light to another, through pockets of darkness, aware that upstairs the parents were asleep.

In the den, there was one light on, a lamp with a cream-coloured shade, on a side table, to the right of the sofa, near the door. He'd seen that light on at night when he happened to drive past the house. It was the same light he remembered from the last time he was in the room.

They stood by a desk in the corner, covered with neat stacks of books, things that interested her father; art, photography, travel, and he uncorked the wine, pouring them each a glass.

"Cheers," he said, and they clinked glasses, both aware of how sharp that sound was in the silent repose of the house.

"Cheers," she said.

The wine had flavour and it had no edges and it went down his throat like honey.

"This must be why they called wine the nectar of the gods," he said. "I never knew what that expression meant until now."

"It is quite remarkable," she said.

"So much of what I drink is just a means to an end."

"What end?"

"You know, a little buzz, a little numbness."

"My husband used to say the same thing. He'd sit up in his studio and drink beer and watch TV while everyone else was asleep. He couldn't face the night without numbing it down. I started to think it might have something to do with him and me."

"It probably did. I think it's all about loneliness and sadness. I think we all ache for love, for the kind of love that is as easy as laughter. We don't want relationships, we don't want to work at this stuff, we just want the contact, the heat and an unimpeded flow."

"I don't know. It must be a male thing. There are so many nuances of love. Children, parents, friends. There is no one person that can make everything right."

"Maybe not," he said, "but it is what men crave, and when the barriers between us and our partners, our lovers, our mates, set in with time, then we start to drink."

He poured them each another glass of wine. They were still standing by the desk.

"Do you remember what happened the last time we were in this room?" she asked.

"Yes," he said.

"What?"

"We were making out, on a Friday night, after seeing a movie, and for the first time we ended up completely naked and I was lying on top of you and I found the safe I always kept in my wallet and I put it on and you crossed your legs at the ankle and said no."

"Then what?"

"Then we stopped kissing and I felt a little ashamed that things had gone so far. And we got dressed. And then I never saw you again."

"That was very hurtful."

"I paid a big price. There's hardly a day goes by that I don't think of how beautiful you looked sitting up in that lamplight. Your tits, your nipples, your belly. It's a vision I can't shake. I know what your cunt smells like and your skin with lake water on it in the sun. I know the little sideways look of pleasure you would give me in the car. I know that you are unique and that no one has ever excited me in a physical way like you."

"You're telling the truth, aren't you?"

"It's always there."

"It's not love, is it?"

"I don't know. I never thought it was. There was an emotional, intellectual dimension that was missing. The stuff that used to cling to my viscera. But I don't sit up at night and long for forgotten conversations about Jung and art history, or for teary confessions about infidelity and other hurts and betrayals, but after twenty-five years I still ache for you."

"You could have forced me. You forced me to do everything else. I mean, I needed to be led, nice girls like me, didn't just admit to wanting sex. Why do you think I made it so hard for you and was never mad after you wrestled me into submission."

"I couldn't do that, even though I was pretty persistent about copping a feel or getting my hand into your pants. And outside of the heat of the moment, I always thought that if I had sex with you I'd have to marry you. I was nineteen. I didn't want to be married. There was a life unfolding. I was figuring it out for myself. It had promise. You weren't the girl for the life I wanted. You were straight when everything interesting was getting a little bent. You were a virgin though. The last one I ever knew."

"I was very close to having sex with you. I loved you. But, as much as I wanted to, I'd been taught that girls like me didn't just give it away."

"You were three years younger than me. Some of the girls my age were beginning to have different ideas."

"You were a virgin too. I could tell."

"Technically not. I'd had some experience but none of it had been without worry or inspired confidence."

"And what about now?"

"Now I could make you come in a thousand ways."

She took a sip of her wine.

"And you?"

"I've only slept with two men. I come infrequently. My husband has been behaving badly for the last few years."

He took a sip of wine and poured what remained of the bottle evenly into both of their glasses.

She put her glass down and came to stand beside him.

"So wha'dya wanna do tonight, Marty?" she said, brushing him with her shoulder.

"I dunno," he said, taking her hand, their fingers interlocking.

"I dunno eitha."

They leaned against the desk, holding hands for a long time, and then he went home.

CHAPTER EIGHTEEN

He decided to walk. It was after three. Forest Hill Village was turned in on itself with only an occasional barking dog breaking the silence and he felt like an intruder on these streets of copious material excess even though he'd grown up just two blocks from where he walked. His life had been pared down in so many ways.

At the corner of Vesta and Ardmore a police car pulled up beside him. The cop rolled down the window.

"Where are you going?" he asked.

Ben kept walking and the car stayed right beside him.

"Look, there's been a robbery, don't make this hard on yourself."

"I'm going home."

"Where do you live?"

"Roxborough."

"Where are you coming from?"

"A friend's."

"Where's your friend live?"

"On Vesta."

"Do you have some ID?"

"No."

"Have you been drinking?"

"That's why I'm walking. Is there a law against that?"

"Get in the car!"

"Why?"

"You meet the description of a prowler that's been seen in the neighbourhood."

"Look, I'm telling you I was at a friend's."

"Let's go back there and confirm that then."

"Fuck, what is the matter with you. I grew up around the corner. I teach at the St. Simon school."

"You're a teacher?"

"Yes."

"Get in the car."

"There's no law that says I have to get in the car. I could call twenty lawyers who live within five blocks of here."

"A few minutes or a few hours. Your choice."

"Asshole."

Ben got into the back seat like getting into a cab, only once seated he saw there were no door handles. He felt trapped and claustrophobic.

The cop swung the car around.

"It's the house on the corner," Ben said.

"This one?"

"Yes."

Leaving the motor running, the cop got out of the car and opened the back door for Ben. They went up the walk together and the cop rang the bell. The den light was still on. It took a few minutes for someone to respond. It was Ellen. She was in a white terrycloth robe with her father's initials embroidered on the pocket.

"Sorry to bother you," the cop said. "Do you know this man?"

"Do I know him? Depends on what you mean by know."

"Look, lady, it's late."

"Yes, I know him. What's going on, Ben?"

"Nothing."

"There's been some break-ins."

"Am I free to go now?"

"Did he just leave your house?"

"Yes."

"Okay. Sorry. Can I give you a ride home?"

"Only if I can sit in the front?"

"No. That's against regulations."

"I'll walk then. How about a note in case I get stopped again?"

"Sorry."

"Ben, come in for a second," Ellen said.

"I could use a drink of water."

"Goodnight, then," the cop said.

"Yeah."

In the house they went into the kitchen.

"Here," she said, offering him a glass of water.

"Thanks. Those pricks have all the power," he said, feeling a little catch in his throat and a pounding in his chest like his heart was tearing at its moorings.

"I'll get dressed and drive you home."

"We just drank a bottle of wine. I'll walk."

"You sure?"

Her hair fell out of a loose knot and across her face. He instinctively reached over and pushed it behind her ear. She caught his wrist and turned toward him. They kissed. There was nothing else they could do. They kissed for a long time. His heart hadn't slowed down, it rocked against his ribs. He held her, trying to catch his breath. Her robe opened, the belt dropped to the floor. He touched her breast and she moaned softly in his ear. She was the only girl who'd ever expressed real pleasure when her breasts were touched. It was a sound from his primordial past and her three children and twenty-five years hadn't changed its timbre. She turned away from him and leaned her head back onto his shoulder, kissing his neck, and he held her breast in one hand, her vagina in the other, stroking forgotten chords, Ellen poised and balanced on her toes, her sounds resonant with his touch, weightless and without force or pressure her labia unfolding, opening, his fingers passing over her clitoris, like a whisper, "Oh Ben, Oh Ben, Oh God, Oh God, Oh," and reaching back she undid his pants and they fell around his knees and she leaned forward against the counter and he fucked her from behind hardly moving at first with the recognition of being inside her then with increased force his thighs slapping against her buttocks and she called out, in the silence of the house, their bodies lit by the light above the stove, "Oh yes, Oh yes, more, more, more, Oh God, Oh God, yes, yes, yes," and he called out and his knees shook when he came and she turned to him and kissed him and made him lie down on top of her on the floor and they made love again savouring everything, and she said, biting the lobe of his ear, "That's three, only nine hundred and ninety-seven to go."

And that's how they were when Mrs. Roberts came down to see what all the ruckus was about.

"You know, Ben Calder, I never liked you," she said, looking at his bare ass, his pants around his ankles, shoes and socks still on, lying on top of her daughter.

"Oh Christ," Ellen said, trying to suppress a laugh, her arms clasped around him, not letting him move.

Having gone to the other side, she was still in the throes of pleasure and was not going to give it up for her mother.

"Now I think you should leave, Ben," Mrs. Roberts said.

"Mother," Ellen said, turning her head in her mother's direction, looking up at her from the kitchen floor, "get out of here right now."

"We'll talk about this later," Mrs. Roberts said.

"We certainly will," Ellen said.

"It's a good thing for the both of you that Mr. Roberts is confined to a wheelchair," Mrs. Roberts said, before leaving the room.

Ellen eased her grip on Ben.

"The first time I have sex with a man other than my husband, in twenty-two years of marriage, I get caught by my mother."

"It could be worse. It could be your husband, or your daughter," he said, standing and pulling up his pants.

"It's like my friend Lorna, getting pregnant the very first time she had sex," she said.

It was four-thirty a.m. on the kitchen clock.

"I better get going," he said.

"Wait. I'll get dressed and walk you part way."

"But it's so late."

"That's okay."

She got up and tied the robe around her waist.

"Don't leave," she said, "I'll be right down."

"God, you're beautiful," he said.

"It's the post-coital haze. In the light of day I'm just some old broad you wouldn't look at twice."

She took the stairs two at a time and returned in running shoes, a hooded sweatshirt and jeans.

"Let's blow this pop stand," she said, opening the door.

Outside, the morning light was something they could sense but couldn't quite see. It was almost five. She took his hand.

"I haven't been out this late in years," he said.

"Me too. Let's walk past your old house."

"It just sold for a million-five. My parents bought it for thirty-nine. I could never live in a house like that now."

They walked west on Elderwood, toward Glenayr.

"Sometimes, I'd walk over to your house early in the morning and just sit on the curb, across the street, knowing you were in your room, breathing in there, asleep, surrounded by your black furniture and your Old Spice cologne. I loved that smell on you."

"You were stalking me."

"You don't wear anything anymore," she said, sniffing the air around them.

"No."

"One night I threw stones at your window. But you'd already gone away to school. And after that first Thanksgiving, when you came home and you didn't call, I knew we were really through and it hurt so bad."

"Look at what they've done," he said, as they neared the house, "they cut down the tree and turned the lawn into a fucking parking lot."

"It's so they can park the Mercedes in front as a testament to their wealth. My husband is an architect. He used to talk about the willful arrogance of the rich. About how they destroyed the visual integrity of the neighbourhood worrying about their own selfish needs. By the time he left he thought they were all a bunch of fucking jerks and refused to finish work on two houses. His reputation suffered. But he was sick of being ignored and treated like shit. These people would hire him for his vision and then argue with everything he said."

"From all I've heard he sounds like an interesting guy."

"He is."

"So?" he said, holding up their entwined fingers.

"So? You and I go back to a time before Casey. You and I have nothing to do with him."

"I don't. But you have a great deal to do with him."

"For twenty years I never even thought about another man. Then he fucked some girl in Italy. I got over it but then he decided he had to see her again. He thought he might be in love with her. So he left me and the kids in Montefioralle and went to Venice for a few weeks. I thought, fuck you mister, you're going to pay for this no matter what happens."

They turned on Burton heading toward Spadina. It was dawn and being up was like being in Paris or Rome, a place you'd been to but not long enough to have exhausted the experience or the anticipation of what remained of the day.

"He's changed," she said, "since quitting architecture and the routine we had here. He's become a sculptor. He doesn't deny himself anything any more. It's partly his age but so what. Most days now I feel I could take a pass on it all."

"The kids?"

"The kids, Casey, Italy. It's my turn to do things for myself," she said, and gave his ass a whack. They were on

Spadina and she jumped on his back. He carried her for twenty yards then put her down and they hugged and kissed beside the road. A few cars drove by and someone honked. It was Saturday morning and though it was late October there was still warmth in the rising sun. He was getting an erection and she pushed up against him like when they were teens.

"Will I see you later?" she asked.

"I think so."

"What about your girlfriend."

"She's working. Shooting a movie."

He looked at his watch.

"She has a rehearsal at eight in the morning."

Nothing in the Village was open. An Ace Bakery driver left baguettes in front of Genua and the Kitchen Table. Ellen walked with him as far as St. Clair. They hugged and kissed on the corner. She turned back up Spadina and he cut across Winston Churchill Park, taking a shortcut home. Gemma would be waiting for him. Worried about how she was going to get to rehearsal on time without him around to look after the kids.

CHAPTER NINETEEN

⋘⋙

At home the living-room light was on. He heard the TV and found Miranda asleep on the sofa, wrapped in a blanket. He turned off the TV and went upstairs. The kids were in their rooms and Gemma was asleep with the duvet half around her waist and half on the floor. She'd had a restless night. He went back downstairs and tidied up the kitchen, rinsing the tomato sauce off the kids' dinner plates and putting them and all the glasses and snack bowls in the dishwasher. He closed the chip bags and put the pop cans and juice boxes out in the recycling bin. It was a lovely, sunny morning now. Miranda was stirring and her eyes opened when he spread the morning paper out on the dining-room table.

"Hi," she said when she saw him, in a voice more sleepy than usual. "You were out pretty late, Mr. C. Did ja have a good time?"

"Yes," he said, walking over to her, trying to talk quietly, "Why are you still here?"

"Your wife came home around two. She didn't have any money. She couldn't pay me or pay for a cab. She figured you'd be home really soon and told me to wait. I called the school. She went to bed and I fell asleep watching a movie."

"Oh Miranda, I'm sorry."

"That's okay. It's six-thirty now. You owe me for thirteen hours. That's seven times thirteen, that's . . ."

"Ninety-one dollars."

"Wow. That's good."

"Okay. Get up now. I'll buy you a coffee on our way to the car. There's a bank machine as well. I guess I'll have to explain to the Dean of Residence why you were out all night."

"She's pretty cool."

He was hoping he could get out of the house before Gemma woke up.

"I'll just pee," Miranda said, throwing off the blanket and standing up.

"Good. Thanks for sharing that with me."

"Do you have a toothbrush I could use?"

"No. Sorry."

At the bank machine, at Marlborough, across from Patachou, she said, "For another fifty bucks, I'll blow you."

His heart sank.

"Thanks, Miranda, but with the kind of night I just had that won't be necessary."

"You're too much, Mr. C."

"Do you do that often?"

"What?"

"Blow guys for money?"

"Sometimes. Cab drivers mostly," she said.

"And what do you do with the money?"

"I don't know. I buy clothes. Drugs. Pot, mostly. Sometimes we smoke a little H."

"Heroin?"

"Yeah."

Heroin was always something he'd wanted to experience but he thought he had better not mention it or she'd show up at his office, after school one day, ready to deal.

He bought them both coffee and doughnuts at the Walker Avenue Coffee Time and then drove her back to school.

"Your kids are sweet," Miranda said. "You can ask me to sit again."

The assistant dean of Residence, Gloria Deacon, was on duty. He and Gloria were friends and on occasion talked about her doctoral thesis on Cézanne and the violent sexual imagery in his early paintings. She had been working on it for six or seven years. The school had been concerned about Miranda but it was not the first time she had been out all night.

"And Ben," Gloria said, "she'd signed out with you, so we knew everything was alright."

"Thanks," he said. "See you Monday."

CHAPTER TWENTY

At home Gemma had just gotten out of the shower. Her hair was wrapped up in a white towel twisted like a turban. Another towel covered her body. He had his pants and shirt off and was standing in his underwear and socks when she came into the room.

"That's a great look," she said. "When'd you get home?"

"A while ago. I took Miranda out for a doughnut and coffee before dropping her off at school."

"That's too bad. My rehearsal's not until ten. I thought we could walk to Patachou and get some breakfast."

"I'll take a quick shower and we can go. Tell the kids to get ready."

"Let's leave them. It's just for an hour and we'll only be a few blocks away."

"Okay."

In the bathroom he could smell Ellen all over him. Sweet and earthy, a little musty, but not fishy or pungent. He washed his hair and his body, quietly elated. Sex with Ellen could have been terrible, depressing, a reminder of how you can never go back. But it wasn't.

Gemma came into the bathroom to get her hair dryer.

"Is that what you call a quick shower?"

"I'll be finished in a second."

The dryer started up and his thoughts stopped dead. It was a grating frantic sound. He stepped out of the shower onto the matt. She was sitting on the edge of the vanity drying her hair.

"Remember when the kids were little and we used to do it in here just to have a little privacy?"

"Yeah."

"I loved that," she said. "The quickie. So satisfying. Come here."

They'd had passive passionless sex three or four times in the last month. This morning, she ached with desire. Woman's intuition. She sensed something was amiss and this was a test, a confirmation. She opened her legs and he moved toward her. She touched his cock and his balls and when he was erect she guided him inside her. She held him by the buttocks, her thighs resting on his hip bones, and they rocked together and they kissed and teased each other's lips with teeth and tongue and he, not about to come any time soon, took some pleasure in the distance he felt between them even as she grew more fluid, liquid in her motion, cursing his name, as was her habit when she came. "Benny. Benny. You fuck you fuck you fuck, Benny." And then he came and started shaking with the release while she held him in her arms, and he cried a river of tears flowing down the channel between her breasts, across her belly, into the delta of her pubic hair. She held him for a few minutes and then loosened her grip. There was only so much time left until she had to leave for rehearsal and they hadn't had breakfast yet.

"You fucked your old friend, didn't you?"

"No," he lied. "It's fatigue and the distance between us. These last few months have been hard."

"Let's get something to eat," she said. "You'll feel better after you eat."

"That's what my mother would say."

She released him and stood on the floor wiping herself dry with a towel. He washed his face. They got dressed and walked over to Patachou. There were two or three other couples on the terrace. The rest of the crowd was inside. He and Gemma each ordered a bowl of cafe au lait and a croissant. His body absorbed the caffeine taking it into every pore. He perked right up.

"See," she said, "I was right. I played a Jewish mother in a local production of *Fiddler* when I lived in Sault Ste. Marie."

"Oh, that must have been great. There isn't a Jew for a thousand miles."

"Yeah, and that's the way we like it."

They finished breakfast without airing any of what was between them. It was enough to spend an hour together, sitting out at a cafe in the sunshine, which had been her idea all along. It was only action that mattered. Words were too easy to contrive.

She got up to leave and they embraced on the terrace.

"I'll be home around six. Let's take the kids out tonight."

"Okay. I'll see you then," he said, and went in to pay the bill.

At home Alex was watching cartoons and Franny was reading a book on the floor.

"We got your note," Alex said, "but we don't think it's fair that you leave us alone like that."

"Gemma and I needed a little time together and here, I brought you each two *pain au chocolate*. Enjoy them. I'm going up to lie down for a while."

The phone rang at noon. He reached for it instinctively. He was groggy and disoriented.

"Hi," a voice said, "it's me. Ellen."

"Oh hi."

"Did I wake you?"

"No. I was just lying here."

"Did you get home alright, without incident?"

"Yeah. You?"

"Walking up Spadina at six in the morning I felt like a kid again," she said.

"I drifted home through the park and there was a clarity to things that I hadn't seen in a long time. The edges of buildings, the blue sky," he said.

"But then I slept and woke and had a fight with my mother and the reality of my situation was clear," she said.

"I found the babysitter still here. On the way to the car she offered to suck my cock for money. What is the reality of your situation?"

"I'm not a person that can chose pleasure over pain. I've always been accepting of my life, positive and uncom- plaining. I've been a supportive wife and put up with a great deal of hurtful behaviour from my husband over the years. Lately it has just gotten worse. He's delusional and thinks his actions haven't rocked the foundations of our family. Being with you last night reminded me of how I was once in love. A love that was total and unqualified. I loved being with you last night and the sex was great and I could stick around and be with you for a week or a month or a year and then what?"

"I don't know," he said.

"That's why I'm leaving on Tuesday and I'd like to see Wanita's art work before I go. I can't do it tomorrow. How about today?"

"My kids have soccer at one and two. I could pick you up at four."

"It would be better if I meet you there."

"The Heath Street door."

"The Heath Street door at four."

"Yeah."

"Ben," she said.

"What?"

"You know you'll get bored, restless."

"I can't promise I won't."

"Why would I risk the well-being of my sons and my daughter for your inability to promise? For the inevitability of love going stale?"

"I would like to be able to love somebody again with all my heart. I would like to break out. I would like to promise."

"People act on much less than I'm feeling, all the time," she said.

"How did you become so afraid? You've only been with one man."

"There was you. Don't forget. I loved you when I was still innocent. And then twenty years of Casey. One person can twist you up in a million ways. And only make you come in one. What's your story? You were afraid when you were young? You had no innocence?"

"I'm not sure about that. I was in love with you. I ached for you. I lay awake at night and shook. I had feverish dreams You were all I could see for months. But there was no flow. Mentally or physically. No connection. No hook."

"You just wanted to put your penis in my vagina."

"I know. But there was more to it than that. It was about aesthetics. It was Beauty with a capital B. You embodied all that I longed for, all my yearning and desire. The ache was religious."

"It was all physical."

"Yes, but it has stayed with me through everything. What's that?"

"Obsessive compulsion, I think it's called."

"Maybe."

"What would have bound you to me once your desire was satisfied?"

"I don't know. Guilt."

"Not much to build a life on."

"It worked in my family. I'll see you at four. I've got to get the kids ready."

"I'd love to meet them."

"We'll see how the afternoon shapes up."

"Okay. Bye."

CHAPTER TWENTY-ONE

The kids were in much the same place he left them.

"Get ready for soccer," he said, "while I make you some lunch."

He considered love and the children. With Alex, his love was total and unqualified. It was clear, direct, and open. Some progress there. For Franny though, it was different. She wasn't his child and there was always the chance that one day she would be gone. He had to protect himself against her going, her turning on him or being turned by her mother. Anything could happen there. With Gemma, it was and always had been day to day.

"Dad, we have to go," Alex said, running down the stairs in his uniform. "My game starts in fifteen minutes. It's the semis. I can't be late."

"Okay. Bring your sandwich and let's go. Are you ready, Franny? Got your cleats, your shin pads?"

"Yes. Why don't you ask Alex? He's more likely to forget them than I am. You just ask me because I'm a girl."

"Oh sweetie, that's not true."

"Yes, it is," she said.

It was five minutes to Rosedale Park, up Roxborough Drive, past a small house he liked, but could never afford.

The owners had put up handwritten signs asking motorists to slow down. He ignored them and was yelled at by an irate woman with a baby in a stroller and a golden lab on a leash.

"Asshole!" she shrieked.

"Dad, we have time," Alex said.

At the top of the hill he turned left on Highland and found a parking spot near the end of the park.

Alex got out and ran to join his team, which was taking practice shots, and Franny stayed with him, standing on the sidelines until a few members of her team showed up.

He loved Ellen. She was the one. He should open the door and invite her in and never let her leave. But he couldn't. Even now, thirty-six years later, on a cool October day in Rosedale Park, he stood in the hallway outside his mother's bedroom door, listening to her speak about her lover and her plans to leave her husband and take the children with her. The moment as vivid as the day it happened, like the heat of the sun focused through a lens, searing a single dot, a period, at the core of his being. A bad marriage and years of borderline alcoholism had done nothing to help.

Alex scored ten minutes into the half, putting his team up by one.

"Thata boy," Ben yelled.

"Your son's playing well," said a dad he'd seen at soccer over the years.

"It's starting to come together."

"My name's Tyler Broadhearst."

Why today?

"Ben Calder," he said, extending his hand.

"Oh, you're Mr. Calder, Mr. C. My oldest daughter's in your Grade Nine class. I thought you looked familiar."

They had been standing on the sidelines at Rosedale Park for five years and their kids had even played on some of the same teams and this was the first time they spoke.

"Maggie. She's a very good art student."

"She loves art but what can she do with it?"

"I don't know," Ben said, wanting out of the conversation.

"No, seriously."

"Seriously, open your eyes, man, and don't stand here insulting what I do when all I want is to watch my son play soccer."

Art was so marginal. At St. Simon's and in the broader culture. He couldn't stand it any more.

"Sorry, Tyler, it's been a rough day," he said.

"Hey, I understand," Tyler said, waving to a woman across the field.

Alex took a pass at mid-field and worked his way up through the defenders, looking for a teammate near the goal. There was no one, so he carried the ball himself, taking a low shot the goalie stopped with a diving catch.

"Great try, Alex," Ben shouted, and a great save, he thought, applauding with the other parents.

Alex's team won the game and advanced to the finals. Alex scored two of the team's three goals. After the handshakes and the high-fives he went home with a friend and Ben watched Franny's game.

It was a tense match with many scoring opportunities going wide or hitting the post. In the end, Franny had one assist with a lovely pass across the crease to a player who tapped the ball into what was virtually an open net. She'd always had good soccer instincts and was able to follow the play and see patterns emerging on the field. Even the boys on her team gave her a lot of respect, and with a penalty shot she was often the one chosen to shoot. That goal was all it took to win and when the whistle blew her team erupted into whoops and cheers of delight. Next week it would be Alex playing Franny for the championship.

Franny wanted ice cream after the game. Ben stopped at Greg's, on Bloor Street, and Franny ran in for two scoops of butterscotch ripple. She didn't want to go to St. Simon's with him but he was reluctant to leave her at home alone for the second time in a day.

CHAPTER TWENTY-TWO

Ellen and Wanita arrived a few minutes late. Ben and Franny were sitting on the curb eating ice cream. The wind was gusting now and blowing the leaves off the trees. Ellen parked the Lincoln in a tight spot beside them. Ben stood up to greet her. She got out of the car and they embraced.

"In Italy," she said, "we never get to experience this kind of autumn. And you must be Franny. This is Wanita."

"Hi," Wanita said.

She and Ben kissed on both cheeks.

"We'll have to stop doing this after your mother leaves. What would your classmates say?"

"How about in the privacy of your office," she asked, "behind that big heavy door?"

"That would be worse."

"With you and Mom, such old friends, I feel like we're practically family."

"Just don't start calling me Uncle Ben."

They moved through the playground to the security door and rang the bell. The guard on duty buzzed the door opened and they entered an enclosed foyer. At the glass booth, with its TV monitors and computer screens, they had to sign in before proceeding any further into the building.

Security was tight since the school became involved with the Sheik of Barhouti. There was a thought that a royal princess might attend St. Simon's and the royals, amongst the world's wealthiest families, worried about crime and corruption. In trying to put them at ease, hoping for a large contribution toward the endowment fund, St. Simon's never mentioned the enslaved children used as camel jockeys in their country, nor the Middle East terrorism Barhouti was known to support. There were security cameras in the hallways, recording the comings and goings of all visitors and the dressing and undressing of the students at their lockers. There were TV monitors mounted on ugly metal frames in classrooms and along the corridors and an alarm system that talked incomprehensibly, built into a new phone system that hardly ever worked. The fear of one princess being kidnapped was changing the culture of openness and trust that had characterized St. Simon's since its inception. These days there wasn't an organization left that wouldn't sell its soul for an infusion of oil money. There was no vision, no depth, no real character left in the corporate model that drove everything, including the schools.

Entering the art studio, on a weekend, lit only by north light, silent, and clear of the materials that usually cover all visible surfaces, with its vaulted ceiling and ancient plaster replicas of classical sculpture, with the quiet aftermath of a week's creative frenzy still lingering in the atmosphere, it felt almost sacred, like entering a dusky chapel in a medieval town in France. Ellen sensed it right away.

"You're lucky to work in a space like this," she said.

"Let me show you around. Franny, if you're bored you can paint or draw. Wanita will get you whatever you want."

There was a small studio down a narrow passageway off the main studio.

"This used to be my office and a store room," he said, "but we needed the space for the students."

She was standing beside him and they looked at each other and then they were kissing.

"Well, is there more to see?" she asked, stepping out of his embrace.

"When my erection subsides we can go into the other studio and I can show you the darkroom."

"Where's Wanita's work?"

"It's in her portfolio."

"Let's see it," she said, and turned into the passageway.

He waited a moment before following her, fussing with some paper, straightening books on shelves.

Wanita had Franny painting a small still-life arrangement she'd set up to draw. Franny was using crayon and water-colours. Both of them were immersed in the work.

He found Wanita's portfolio and opened it up on a table near the window.

"These are the first things she did," he said, indicating some uncertain drawings of student models. "I think it was the first day she arrived."

He turned the pages and the drawings became bolder with lines less hesitant.

"These are gorgeous," Ellen said. "I'm amazed. She's never shown any proclivity for this. Her father went to art school and he could really draw. But not like this."

"She's so young and these are only the beginning."

"How did this happen?" Ellen asked. "She hasn't even been here a month."

"I don't know. It was there all the time. She just had to get into a situation where it could come out. The change, being away from home, boarding school, competitiveness, all worked as a catalyst."

"For someone who never wanted this job, you're pretty good at it."

They were standing hip to hip, touching, moving against each other, riding a wave of desire that rolled between them. She moved away. One step. Then another.

"Well, what do you think?" Wanita asked, coming between them, putting her arm around her mother.

"I think they're beautiful. You're so talented. Your father should see these."

"He's bound to visit, sometime," Ben said.

"No. I don't think so," Ellen said.

"He will if I ask," Wanita said.

"I wouldn't bet on it," Ellen said.

"Why? Is there stuff you're not telling me?"

"We'll talk about it later."

"I'll draw you, Mom, and you can take that home to Dad."

"I don't think I'd be such a good model."

"All you have to do is sit here," Ben said, indicating a stool on the model stand behind them.

"A half-hour pose, Mom, that's all. A girl in my class did a series of nude studies of her mother."

"Oh, okay," Ellen said.

"Sit three-quarters to us," Ben said.

She adjusted her position.

"That's good," he said, "we can see the lovely structure of your face."

"What's left of it," she said.

Wanita worked standing up, drawing on a large sheet of heavy paper using an assortment of pencils.

"This is hard," she said, after a few minutes.

"Don't think about how your mother's going to like the rendering. Just do it as you see it, Ben said."

Franny came into the studio. She was feeling left out and when she saw what Wanita was doing she wanted to do the same thing.

Ben helped her set up an easel and clip her paper to a drawing board. He looked over at Ellen. She was wearing a black T-shirt, blue jeans and low boots with elastic sides. He could see the gold ankle bracelet she used to wear in high school. It wasn't there last night. Her face, in this light, was etched with fine lines around her eyes and her mouth, lines of good nature, from laughing and smiling, and view-ing her world with patience and love. She lifted her hand to scratch her neck. A few strands of hair fell across her eyes.

"Mom, don't move," Wanita demanded.

Ben got a sketchbook from his office. He didn't draw yesterday. It was the first day he missed in almost a year.

Ellen's face had aged but to him it hadn't changed. As a young girl there had been something a little coarse, a lit-tle adult about her face. Now it was as if she had grown into it. Drawing required him to be objective, outside the subject, so he could see it clearly, analytically. In choosing only to draw from life he had chosen to eliminate expres-sion and imagination. He had also chosen to eliminate colour. Colour (paint) can be so seductive. Colour was the hook the artist working the carny midway used to pull the viewer into his tent. Ben had no hook. All he had was a few thousand pages of drawings. Subtle, obsessive, renderings of things that came into his line of vision. The drawings, like the one of Ellen he just finished, were heartbreaking in their delicacy.

Forty-five minutes passed and Ellen had to move. It had begun to grow dark in the room. Wanita kept working, softening the cleft below the nose. Ben stood behind her. Her drawing was inspired. She was in a zone all by herself. She could hardly speak. The process was like some kind of religious ecstasy.

Franny came over to look.

"Wow," she said, "that's really good. I wish I could do that."

"Your piece is lovely," Ben said.

"It's baby stuff," she said, and crumpled it into a ball.

Ellen came off the stage and over to look at Wanita's drawing.

"Oh Franny, your work was so expressive and rich in tone. It had so much energy," Ben said.

"Energy, shmenergy. I want to draw something that looks like something."

"Okay," he said, moving over to where she stood, "we'll work on that."

"No we won't. Alex and I know. It's only a matter of time until you and Mom break up."

"Oh honey, that's not true," he said, putting his arms around her and hugging her.

Ellen gave Wanita a kiss on the cheek and said how moved she was by the quality and the sensitivity of her drawing. Wanita shrugged it off and said, "You know Franny, you can hang out with me sometime. I can help you with your drawing and we can talk about men, Dads and how little you can really expect from them."

"That's certainly been my experience," Franny said.

"Mine too," said Wanita.

CHAPTER TWENTY-THREE

❦

Later, Ben and Gemma took Franny and Alex to Bar Italia for dinner. The place was crowded, noisy, jumping in its way. They sat in the front, near the window, and he watched the street — much quieter now than during the summer. Gemma was feeling cheerful. The rehearsals were going well and she was starting to get a good feeling for the film, like it might actually get released and be seen. She was counting on this role to bring her some attention so that getting the next part might not be so hard. She was emphasizing her skill in this role, not just her body. But this was Canada and one good thing, one success in the arts, didn't lead to another. He listened to her and thought about Ellen. He did a mental inventory of her body. Images from the distant past merged with the most recent. He ate pasta with grilled chicken in a spicy tomato sauce.

"So both kids won their games today," Gemma said.

"Yes. And Alex played brilliantly, scoring twice for his team. And Franny set up the winning goal for hers, with a pass across the goal crease. It was very exciting."

"I should be able to make the final next week. We start shooting on Wednesday but the weekends are off."

"That's great," he said.

"As if you really care."

"Of course I do."

"Alex," she said, "I went to school with Patrick's mother. We were pretty good friends until Grade Eight."

Patrick was the boy Alex went home with after soccer. Ben knew Patrick's mother as well. She had a daughter at St. Simon's. Since teaching there, Ben knew about ten thousand women in Toronto and Felicia Timmins was one of the phoniest, old fashioned snobs he had ever met.

"Was that at Havergal?"

"Yes."

"Didn't Felicia grow up on Melrose or somewhere?"

"Old Orchard Grove, actually."

"Oh yes, The Grove. In a three-bedroom bungalow built just after the war."

"The big war," she said, "WW2."

"Right. They built better bungalows after that one. Felicia's bungalow was built by Italians. They built the Coliseum you know," Ben said.

"Her father owned a hardware store on Avenue Road."

"And from working there after school she developed a British accent as thick as a tub of margarine."

"No. That's from the Royal Academy of Dramatic Arts."

"And what did she do with it?"

"Summer stock, in Lindsay. Two seasons."

"And married a local boy."

"A young doctor, actually, who summered in the region."

"She called me about a week ago and blamed me for her daughter getting paint on her uniform. She said it was the third time it happened and they didn't have the money to be replacing uniforms endlessly. I said we had aprons for all the students and her daughter chose not to wear one because it wasn't cool. Well, I should make her wear one, she said, it's my responsibility. And she wanted the school to pay for replacing the skirt. All this in that lofty accent, and then she complained about the mark her daughter got in art last year. I said a B was a pretty good mark and she said there should be no B's in art."

"Just B movies."

"Dad," Alex said, "this is B for boring."

"You and Mom do this all the time," Franny said. "You just start talking about some dumb thing and go on and on like Alex and I weren't even here."

He knew she was right.

And Gemma knew it as well.

"It's just that Ben and I haven't seen each other all day," Gemma said.

"I know," Franny said.

"It's a way that Ben and I connect," Gemma said.

"Like foreplay," he said, "something you will understand when you're older."

"Ben, that's not necessary," Gemma said.

"Oh, fuck it," Ben said, and got up and left the table.

He went out onto the street and started walking west on College, past the Diplomatico, Cocco Lezzone, and other spots on the street. All were crowded. He walked past the Portuguese grocers and the depressing little sports cafes where a few old men sat and watched some insignificant soccer match on television. He walked as far as Crawford Street and turned around. The Sicilian Ice Cream Parlour was empty. He was angry and frustrated. It felt like the kind of irrational rage that happened when he first quit smoking.

Just sitting there below the surface like some piece of materiel that hadn't exploded when it was fired and was triggered by a comment or a tone of voice or the look on someone's face. Smoking had left him littered with mercurial debris, little blasting caps that could set off his unsettled, unresolved, emotional residue — garbage he had been carrying around since childhood. He was forty-six but there was still a hurt ten-year-old alive in his being, and that ten-year-old often responded to what was going on in the present. He had smoked to sooth that child and in quitting he left it raw and unattended. Only psychoanalysis could help now but who had the time or the money. Maybe Prozac or Zoloft or some other mood and erection inhibitor. It was too much of a price to pay. When he got back to the restaurant they were gone, and with them the car as well. He was calmer and waded through the crowd to have a quick espresso at the bar.

He called Ellen from the pay phone but hung up before anyone answered. He would just go there. He didn't want to hear any reasons why he shouldn't. All he could do was see Ellen. There was no other option, no other destination. He started walking — east on College and right up Bathurst. Bathurst Street was a hole, a major north-south street in a big city that had remained essentially residential. Tired residential, the kind that happens when the streetcar speeds by old homes that haven't been painted in thirty years. There was a commercial strip between Bloor and Dupont. It was all down-scale with the usual coffee places, neighbourhood bars, picture framers, laundromats, used book and record stores, hair and nail salons and grocers varying from Caribbean specialties to Korean. No place interested him, nothing made him want to return.

From Bar Italia it took about an hour to reach the
Hemingway Apartments, the famous building north of St.
Clair, where Earnest Hemingway had lived for about two
weeks in 1927, while working at the *Toronto Star*. Just north
of that was the Bathurst Street Bridge spanning a deep
ravine. A guy Ben knew jumped off that bridge and died in
the mud below. He struggled to remember his name.
Andrew. Andrew Feldman. He was studying medicine. A
Jewish intellectual with a lot of promise, who thought he
was gay and chose not to live with the consequences. The
night before he killed himself he showed up, uninvited, at
Ben's place, something he had never done before, and made
a pass at Ben's girlfriend in a narrow hallway near the bathroom. She rejected him and he went over to Mark Stella's
place and made a pass at his wife. She rejected him as well
and the next day, or later that night, he jumped. It was the
first suicide in the group and it seemed like such a waste.
It was 1974 or '75. Ben looked over the bridge. It was not
popular with jumpers. Not like the Bloor Viaduct. It didn't
seem that high and the landing was soft. If one was going to
jump, Ben thought, one didn't want to miss and risk a terrible permanent physical disability that would leave one
immobilized, dependant and without choices. Had the fall
killed Andrew or had he drowned in the mud? There was
talk of building a safety net around the Bloor Viaduct to
catch jumpers. But they would go somewhere else. In Toronto there were many venues for suicide and much inspi-
ration.

Just north of the bridge he turned onto Burton Road.
The tree- lined streets of Forest Hill Village offered respite
from the bleak façades of Bathurst Street but not from his

thoughts. With its fine homes the Village was hell in other ways, mentally and emotionally, the way all bastions of privilege tend to be. He walked softly and kept an eye out for the police.

Ellen's house was dark except for the lamp in the den. The curtains were all drawn. He looked at his watch. It was almost eleven. The walk had taken longer than he anticipated. He rang the bell and waited.

"You're lucky it's me," Ellen said, when she answered the door. "My mother really doesn't want to see you around here again."

"I haven't been banned from anyone's house since I shit in a paint can in Warren Frederick's basement, when I was ten."

"Mom said she never thought much of you, and now that she's seen your ass there is no reason to see you at all."

"And what about you?" he said, reaching for her hand and pulling her toward him. She offered no resistance.

"I was just lying in bed wanting you."

They kissed and his fingers found the warm contour of her hip inside her robe.

"I'm glad you're here. I couldn't have waited until tomorrow."

She took a set of car keys off a hook beside the door and led him to the driveway where, until today, her father's old Lincoln, a '78 or '79, had been parked for almost a year. It was a four-door and she got into the back and lay down on the seat, leaving her robe on, letting it fall open. With her legs bent slightly at the knee she spread them apart and touched her vagina with her hand.

"This is where I was when you rang."

He crawled in on the floor beside her and kissed her inner thighs and licked her, lapping at her juices, touching her lips, breathing deeply, inhaling her scent, nuzzling her. She started to hum, a forgotten sound, and he kissed her and teased her with his fingers and his tongue and she tugged on his ears until he was kneeling between her legs and she undid his jeans, pulled them down over his hips and they fucked. It had been many years since either of them had done it in a car, and afterwards they lay beside each other on the narrow seat, looking up at the branches of a tree, the house, a window reflecting a street light that was a stand-in for the moon.

In the back seat of her father's old car he said, "I love you," and he meant it.

"I love you," she said, "and I always have, and I always will but I'm going back to Italy Tuesday, to be with my kids."

"How will we survive?"

"I've lived this long without you, what's another ten or fifteen years?"

"I'm not getting any younger. I don't think I have the strength."

"You'll survive. You always have. You've got Alex to think about and I'm leaving Wanita in your hands. I want you to make sure she stays focused on her art work and gets into a good program next year."

He'd had this conversation with concerned parents before.

"Don't go," he said, rolling on top of her.

"It's not until Tuesday," she said, touching his balls and his cock.

"I know," he said, squeezing her buttocks.

"Oh God," she moaned, getting her legs up around his shoulders, "just fuck me."

And he did, frantically, with the intention to please and to hurt, to leave an imprint, her nails piercing the skin on his hips, the old car rocking on its suspension. After, they were still and he lay down on her with his full weight and pulled the robe around them both. The sweat on their bodies started to cool and the windows dripped with condensation in the late October night.

"Soon," he said, "you won't be able to make a choice."

"I'm past it already," she said, locking her arms around him. "I'm running on willpower and I'm one tough mother."

"Don't leave," he said.

"I have to."

CHAPTER TWENTY-FOUR

He took a cab home at three-thirty in the morning. He opened a bottle of red wine and sat down at the dining-room table. There was a bowl of green bananas on the table. He looked at the bananas and rearranged them in the bowl. Gemma came downstairs in a T-shirt with no bra. He thought about jabbing a sharp pencil through his cheek. She was tense and her nipples were hard. Pain might help him regain his perspective.

"I'm sorry," he said, "for my outburst at the table."

"You should be. Where have you been?"

"Nowhere. I walked on College then went to a bar."

"I don't believe you."

"It's been a rough couple of months."

"It has? Not for me."

"Oh, come on. We've spent a lot of time apart and you've been preoccupied with getting your career going again."

"Nothing's changed in how I feel."

"The kids see the distance, see me making dinner and see you're not at the table. They think we're breaking up."

"Well, we might be if you keep acting like such a prick."

"I'll try to rein it in. You want a drink?"

"No. And you should get some sleep so we can do something fun with the kids tomorrow."

"What were you thinking about?"

"A hike in the ravine, a bike ride, a movie. Something with the four of us."

"Miss Post is looking for a reason to fire me and I feel this sick compulsion to give her one. It's like I can't stop myself."

"It wouldn't be a good time for you to be out of work."

"I know."

"I'm going to bed," she said.

He poured another glass of wine then drew a man with a bunch of bananas where his cock should be. The bananas curved up, graceful and arching. He drew a few women kneeling, peeling the bananas and eating them. To this he added context, a little Tahitian village alluding to Gaugin. When he finished he tore the drawing out of his sketchbook and filed it in a separate folder. Anyone can draw a picture but how many people can draw one every day for eleven years? The words, "Oh God," left his lips. What the fuck was he going to do?

He drew a speeding train. On the track, down a ways, he drew a large black and white cow. The cow stood across the track with its head turned to one side, looking at the train, the way cows do. He then drew himself diving in front of the cow, with an arm raised to alert the train. It was a futile gesture. A Gestalt interpretation would show him that he was the train and the cow, as well as the person, and would help to clarify his dilemma. He tore the drawing out of the sketchbook and filed it with the others. He finished the bottle of wine and lay down beside Gemma.

It had been a long time since he thought about God. Tonight was some Jewish holiday. Sukkot or Shavuot. Maybe he should call his father and go to synagogue with him. He couldn't do that. It was something about the way they all kissed the Torah. He had an aversion to groups of people behaving in a proscribed way. It was so primitive. He had always wanted a transcendent experience. But that was not a part of the religious practice he knew. Had he been missing the point all along? Orthodox Judaism was not about the quality of his experience, it was about faith, about letting go, about giving himself over to another set of rules, another way of approaching life. It was not about searching for meaning or experience, it was about acceptance, about giving up and standing there in the synagogue, praying to God, with his head covered, feeling part of something larger than himself, something that had existed for thousands of years. He would be in a crowd, comfortable in its midst instead of being outside, looking in, with his critical eye. He listened to Gemma breathe beside him. He would return to his roots, give himself over to God, lie down in the river and say Amen. He would take the Lord into his heart, accept Jesus, be born again. He would love freely and the pain and loneliness would go away.

CHAPTER TWENTY-FIVE

Sunday, Alex woke with a stomach ache and found his father fully dressed, asleep on top of the sheets.

"Where does it hurt?" Ben asked.

"Here," Alex said, indicating his entire abdomen.

"Are you hungry?" Ben asked.

"No."

Stomach aches were problematic. There was nothing to see, to poke, to prod, to touch. There was just this internal ache that could, if ignored, be fatal. Alex was a strong kid who had been through a lot, including his mother taking off and disappearing from his life. Occasionally he had some physical upset but not often. He wasn't a child who had frequent sore throats, colds, earaches, or allergies. He didn't bump into things, he didn't trip and fall. The stomach ache continued throughout the morning and Ben became concerned. It could be anything.

Without a doctor who made house calls, the only real alternative for parents in Toronto, other than waiting hours for a practitioner from Med-Visit, was going to emergency at the Hospital for Sick Children. It was an experience everyone dreaded as it involved waiting in an airless room with a crowd of weeping, moaning, coughing, snurfling, puking, screaming, restless children who were not your own. At eleven, Ben took Alex down to the hospital and Gemma and Franny went for a walk.

Alex was quiet and Ben was quiet, worried about his son. The emergency waiting room was more crowded than usual and no one looked familiar to Ben. He signed in and they waited. The other people all looked like they came from somewhere else. The pain did not subside. At two o'clock they finally saw a doctor. An older man with an easy professional manner, calm and reassuring as he performed a thorough examination. Not the usual perfunctory job done by a harassed intern.

"Are there any emotional upheavals in the boy's life?" he asked Ben.

Ben just looked at him.

"How are things at home?" he asked.

"Not as smooth as they have been," Ben said, "but nothing significant has happened."

"You swore at Gemma and left us at the restaurant," Alex said.

The doctor looked at Ben.

"It was just an argument. The kind of thing that happens with couples every day."

"No, Dad. It was the first time that happened with Gemma," Alex said.

How literal-minded kids were.

"There might be a little tension between us, right now," Ben said. "I'm under some stress at work."

"What kind of work do you do?" the doctor asked.

"I teach," Ben said.

"Where?"

"St. Simon's."

"A fine school," the doctor said. "My niece went there. Katie Conroy?"

"A great kid," Ben said, "I taught her art."

"She's in law school now," the doctor added. "Look, there is nothing physically wrong with Alex here that I can see. He is a sensitive boy. Keep him on a diet of plain noodles, rice, no rich or fried foods. Skim milk, clear juices, that kind of thing. If the pain persists, come back and see us. And we have a new family counselling department you might want to look into."

"Thanks, Doctor," Ben said.

Alex was feeling a little better by the time they got into the car.

"How about an ice cream, Dad?"

"You heard the doctor."

"Come on."

"Why not?"

Bland foods and family counselling were not things to which Ben subscribed.

"You have to know, son," he said, "that whatever happens, I love you, and we will always be together."

"I know, Dad. I love you. And I love Franny too. And Gemma."

"It's just a bit of a rough time. Everything will be alright," Ben said, mussing Alex's hair and touching his cheek. Alex was his only child, his only son, and there was no confusion in his loyalty and his love for him.

CHAPTER TWENTY-SIX

Ellen called at six-thirty when he was making dinner. It was burger night and he was dicing garlic to put into the patties. Potatoes, which he'd cut into small cubes, were frying in olive oil, seasoned with thyme.

"Hello," he said.

"Hi. It's me. I cancelled my flight."

"When can I see you?"

"What are you doing now?"

"I'm making dinner."

"Let's take a walk later?"

"I'll meet you at the café, on the corner, at nine-thirty."

"Who was that?" Franny asked, coming into the kitchen to get another carrot stick.

"It was Ellen."

"Wanita's mom?"

"Yeah."

"Why'd she call?"

"Because we're old friends and she lives in Italy and I don't speak to her much. That's why."

"Does she know Mom?"

"No."

He turned to stir the fries then shaped the patties by passing the meat back and forth between his hands. He'd bought some sesame seed buns and he put them in the oven to warm.

"Where's Wanita?" Franny asked.

"She's probably at school."

"It must be strange for her living with a bunch of people."

"It is at first. But you get used to it and figure out ways to make it fun."

"Like what?" Franny asked.

"Oh, friends, clubs, trips, games, things like that," he said, not mentioning recreational drug use and personal Web sites.

The burgers were sizzling in the pan and he drained the fries.

"Franny, could you set the table, please?"

"Why me?"

"You set, Alex will clear."

"Fine."

Gemma came downstairs. He opened a bottle of wine. She talked to the kids about what it was like to uproot and go to school in a new place and learn a new language and make new friends. She had gone to France on an exchange when she was at school.

"I'd like to do that," Alex said.

"Is everything alright, Alex?" Ben asked.

"Yeah. But you know it's October," he said.

"How's your tummy?" Ben asked.

"Fine."

Gemma opened the mustard, relish and ketchup. Ben took the buns out of the oven. And they all sat down at the table and ate. Alex seemed to be ravenous, no sign of discomfort. Still, Ben worried about him.

"Franny told me how perfectly still Ellen sat as a model. Did you draw her?"

"Yes."

"Can I see?"

"It's at school. I'll bring it home tomorrow."

"Franny said Wanita's drawing was fabulous."

"It was."

"You said you'd help me, remember?" said Franny.

"Ben, don't Bogart that wine."

"Mom's been having a hard time with this role," Franny said, "she's finding it difficult to penetrate the character."

"I'm sure the director can help her with that," Ben said.

Gemma shot him a look.

"I'm not sure 'penetrate' is the right word," Alex said, teasing Franny. "I think appropriate is more to the point."

"When did you get so smart?" she said.

"I've always been smart. Just no one listens to me."

"That's not true," Ben said.

"Yes, it is," said Alex, standing up and leaving the table.

"He's just doing that because he doesn't want to clear," said Franny.

"Bitch," said Alex.

"You come back here," said Ben.

"No."

Alex was still anxious and Ben let him stay in his room reading and snuggling with his teddy bears. Ben sat with until close to nine.

Gemma and Franny had cleaned up the kitchen and Gemma had gone up to take a bath. Ben opened the bathroom door to tell her that he was going out for a walk. Gemma was on the phone, sitting with one leg hanging over the edge of the tub. The water flowed softly onto her pelvis, which was arched toward the faucet. She wasn't speaking, just listening with the phone pressed between her shoulder and her ear. Her eyes were closed. She had no sense of his presence and he closed the door without disturbing her.

Franny had settled into a favourite TV show and he had to tell her three times that he was going out.

Ellen wore jeans and a T-shirt, a leather jacket and an old pair of Keds with no socks. Her hair was gathered loosely at the base of her neck. He kissed her on the lips. The café was closed and they started walking south on Yonge Street, holding hands. At Gibson they turned west toward Ramsden Park, walking past the row houses on the north side. The park was empty and they moved along the edge of the hill beside the upper tennis courts and stopped in the shadows of the stone building where players reserved a court by hanging their racquet on a numbered peg. There they kissed and pressed against each other like teenagers. She undid his belt and the zipper of his jeans and got down on her knees.

"I want you to come in my mouth. Before I leave I want you to come in every orifice of my body. I want to go back to Italy full of you and I want to stand and talk to Casey with your cum dripping out of my pores."

Her language alone excited him. How she had changed.

"Oh God!" he shouted, into the cool autumn air, the rustling leaves, as she held him at the back of her throat, sucking then licking him dry.

They continued walking and sat on the swings in the playground at Cottingham School, looking up at the stars, before settling in at the Rosedale Diner for a drink. They both had scotch; Macallan 15-year-old, a great drink after a blowjob. They sat on the same side of the table facing the door and the window, still holding hands, flushed with excitement.

CHAPTER TWENTY-SEVEN

◉

Monday morning Ben dropped Alex off at school. Late, he had less than five minutes to get to his first class. Russell Hill Road was jammed with cars, backed up to Kilbarry, from the light at St. Clair. He punched the steering wheel in frustration. Who would be waiting for him? Grade Ten. They were etching. It involved a nitric acid bath, viscous permanent inks, a press, paper, solvents, setting up and cleaning up before the next class came into the studio. It required vigilance, discipline, foresight to prevent an accident, to contain the chaos. Someone was in his parking spot. The lot was full. He parked on the lawn. It had only been two weeks since he was last reprimanded for that. He grabbed his binder from the back seat and started to run. He knew he would be sweating by the time he reached the third floor.

Racing in the front door, moving toward the receptionist's desk, the receptionist stood up and flagged him down. She was the centre on Miss Post's offensive line.

"Mr. Calder, Miss Post would like to see you in her office."

"I have a class. I'll see her later."

"Now, Mr. Calder."

He knocked on Miss Post's door. It was just ten feet past the reception desk.

"Come in," she said.

He thought about his recent behaviour in the car.

"Is something funny, Mr. Calder?"

"No. But if it was, I'd be sure to share it with the class."

She was sitting behind her desk holding a Mount Blanc fountain pen. It had been a gift from the Chairman of the Board in recognition of the fine work she was doing at St. Simon's. Her legs were crossed at the ankles. She had slender ankles that hinted at more than autogamic possibilities.

"You were supposed to write a two-page rationale on why you should keep your job as Head of the Art Department. Do you have it?"

"No."

"Your not doing that, and the other things I have requested, add up to gross insubordination."

"Although it is beginning to feel like a life sentence, St. Simon's is not a Chinese prison where I have to justify my right to exist with a written statement each day."

"I asked you to do something. I am the leader around here."

She stood up when she said that.

"You might be the boss but you're no leader."

"How dare you speak to me like that," she said, and threw the pen onto her desk for emphasis. The cap was off and the nib exploded, spraying indigo-blue ink onto the documents she was about to sign and the camel-coloured suit she was wearing as well.

He looked at her and turned to leave. He was really late for his first class. She called his name as he closed the door. Fuck her, he thought, and spent the rest of the morning waiting for the axe to fall.

Nothing happened.

In the afternoon, nothing.

At four he went to the human resources office and checked his file. There was a formal letter outlining his insubordination, his refusal to do the things she requested, his not being a team player. There was a blue stain on the corner of the page. She was building her case.

He quickly wrote up his version of what had happened and put it in his file. There had been no action in there for over a year. The last thing was a reprimand for leaving Crazy Sports Day early and his three-page letter in response. The regime made infants out of everyone.

Ellen was staying a few blocks from the daycare and he thought he would go and see her before getting Alex. When he went outside, his car was not there. He found Monica, Head of Security, an otherwise pleasant, hard-working woman, who told him his car had been towed at Miss Post's insistence. Had he not been warned about parking on the lawn?

CHAPTER TWENTY-EIGHT

"Being with you has made me brave," he said to Ellen, talking on his cellphone while standing at the car pound on Cherry Street, in the fading October light. He was waiting for his car. A cold damp breeze blew in off the lake. It was desolate and awful there.

"Or stupid," he continued, telling her about the events of the day.

"Ben," she said, "you ought to be careful about what you say. You could be fired."

"I realized this morning that I don't give a shit. I should have quit a long time ago."

"I need you there, for Wanita."

"She can come with us." .

"Where?"

"Let's take our kids somewhere, get jobs and make a life of it. I don't want to live without you."

"You'll manage. It's just the sex. Wait'll you take a good look at my sagging flesh and prominent veins. You'll be looking for reasons to leave me."

"You are the most beautiful woman I have ever seen. How many times do I have to tell you that?"

"Lots."

"You are the most beautiful woman I have ever seen."

"Love is blind, baby."

"Don't baby me, Momma."

"Don't Momma me, baby."

"Am I going to see you tonight?"

"I don't know. I promised Wanita I'd take her out for dinner."

"Just a second. I have to pay this guy for my car," he said, laying the phone on the counter as he picked up the bill.

"A hundred and eighty dollars! Are you fucking nuts? Cash only? Where I am supposed to get the cash? Parliament Street. Fuck."

"Listen Ellen, I've got to go. I have to walk up to the bank machine on Parliament . . . What do you mean you close in an hour. Oh shit."

"Ben, I'll get Wanita at school and bring you the money. She wanted to eat at Tiger Lily's. You're not too far out of the way."

"You know where I am?"

"Yeah, on Cherry Street. I had to get Casey's car from there after he ran away. I'll see you soon."

"You don't have to do this."

"I'll see you soon."

He looked at the attendant.

"Why so fucking much money?"

"You have to pay for the tow."

He stepped outside and looked through the fence. The western sky was a deep violet. One last tentacle of light reached across and touched the Bank of Nova Scotia tower, igniting it, a beacon of radiant excess. Then it went dark. The building and the horizon at once. The guard dogs started barking. A wind chime rang on the deck of a freighter moored across the street. The name Nowheresville came to mind. Nowheresville and no way back.

Ellen arrived with the money. She and Wanita asked if he'd join them for dinner. He declined, having promised Franny and Alex he'd pick them up after retrieving the car and take them out to a deli up on Bathurst Street. Alex was crying when he came in the door. Franny was trying to comfort him but was not having any success.

Ben hugged him and stroked his hair and asked him what was wrong when the sobs subsided.

"My mother called," he said. "She's in Toronto and wants to see me. She's been here for two weeks and she just called today. She says she's leaving on Friday."

"All in all it's shaping up to be some kind of day. You don't have to see her, you know," Ben said.

"I want to but I'm afraid. Last time I couldn't stop thinking about her for months."

"Fuck it. I'll make the decision for you. You can't see her. She's a cunt and she'll ruin your life."

"Oh Dad. You can't say that. She's my mother," he said, and started crying again.

"You know, I'll bet you passed her on the street or caught her out of the corner of your eye. It's like you knew this was coming and have been anticipating it for weeks now. Where's she staying?"

"With a friend. Here's the number."

He dialed the number.

"Hello," Ben said, "Is Astrid there?"

"Astrid," he said, when she got on the phone, "you can only see him for a short time and with me present."

"How are you, Ben?" she asked.

He'd always liked the sound of her voice. And now more than ever with its hint of a British accent.

"Great. I saw Norton Hammish last Saturday. I hadn't seen him in years."

"Me too."

"It figures. You're probably staying with him and his wife and children."

"No. But I am staying with Marnie and she's something of a mutual friend."

"You know, since psychoanalysis failed you miserably, there are some new drugs on the market that might help."

"Very funny. When can I see Alex?"

"Hold on," he said, covering the mouthpiece with his hand.

"Should we take her out for dinner with us?" he asked the children.

"Okay," Alex said.

"I've never met this person," Franny said.

"You can ignore everyone and just eat."

"Astrid," he said, "I was planning to take the kids out for dinner tonight and you're welcome to come along."

"Okay. I've got plans but I don't suppose we'll be too late."

"No. In and out. Where are you staying?"

"In Rosedale. On Roxborough Drive. Number 128. A red brick place at the top of the hill."

"God, I've always wanted that house. Who are these people?"

"Marnie, you know. She and I used to do some modelling together. She married a guy in the ad business named Terry Mitel."

"Norton's pub-crawling Brit pal."

"You got it. Oh, I'm a totally observant vegetarian."

"No problem. We'll be there in fifteen minutes. If there is any change of plan I'll call."

"Are you sure you're up for this Alex?" he said.

"Yes."

"It's too bad Mom isn't home," Franny said. "She could come along, meet Alex's mom."

"They met once a long time ago," Ben said.

"Funny, she never mentioned it."

"Maybe she forgot," he said. "Now, let's get ready to go."

CHAPTER TWENTY-NINE

Ben parked in the driveway and went to get Astrid. She was waiting at the door as beautiful and stylish as ever. He kissed her on both cheeks.

"You can do better than that," she said.

He hugged her reluctantly and led her to the car.

Alex stood there waiting for her.

"Well, who's this?" she said.

"Oh Mom, you know it's me," Alex said.

She opened her arms to him and he came to her and held her tight.

"Why, you're a man now," she said.

"Not quite."

"Why don't you two ride in the back and Franny will ride up front with me," Ben said. "Franny, come out and say hello."

Franny got out of the car and shook hands with Astrid.

"How do you do," she said, "I'm Franny."

"A pleasure to meet you," said Astrid. "You're still driving this?"

"It goes."

Astrid put her arm around Alex and they talked in the back seat. Ben glanced at her occasionally in the rear view mirror. She was telling Alex how she had a new job working for the British fashion magazine *Vogue* and got to travel to all the fashion shows.

Ben cut through Rosedale and Forest Hill over to Bathurst Street and drove straight up Bathurst to the Palm Deli, north of Wilson. Bathurst was as ugly up here as it was to the south only here there was some commercial life and a series of store-front synagogues offering nuances of devotion that he couldn't even imagine. These synagogues, Hasidic for the most part, were busy until ten or eleven at night and there only seemed to be men going in and out, except on Saturday when their wives and children joined them, and the men, dressed in the traditional finery of black breaches, knee socks, long coats, and spectacular fur hats, looked like they came from another century. One of the fashion designers tried to appropriate the look one season, even adding fake earlocks to the broad brimmed hats, and it was a complete disaster. It was some one who should have known better and when he asked Astrid who it was she couldn't remember.

"Well it wasn't Karl Lagerfeld," she said. "It'll come to me."

He pulled into the parking lot of the 1950s strip-mall and found a place in front of the restaurant. They got out of the car and he couldn't help notice how short Astrid's dress was.

Their favourite table was available and the kids settled into the banquette by the window. He and Astrid sat on chairs facing them. Once, about fifteen years ago, a woman as attractive as Astrid had entered the restaurant. He had definitely forgotten what it was like to be out in public with her.

"This is a deli," she said.

"Yeah."

"I'm a vegetarian."

"They have salads, vegetable soup, potato pancakes. You'll be fine."

The waitress came over to the table, called him 'Hon' as in "What would you like, Hon," touched Astrid's hair and then her shoulder.

"God, you're beautiful," she said. "Where's the actress?"

"She's working tonight."

"Un huh. So, what'll it be?"

"I'll have the chicken fingers and fries," said Franny.

"What's the soup today?" asked Alex.

"Split pea."

"I'll have soup and the sandwich special. Pastrami on rye and french fries," he said.

"And you?" she said, looking at Astrid.

"I'll have a garden salad with oil and vinegar dressing and a potato pancake with apple sauce."

"I'll have soup and the sandwich special, as well," said Ben. "I'd like the meat hand-cut and lean."

"Drinks?"

"Vernors."

"Vernors."

"Club soda."

"Club soda."

"It's too bad you don't eat meat," Ben said to Astrid. "Pastrami doesn't get any better than this."

"I could always count on you to take me to the finest places."

Alex looked at his mother and then looked out the window. It was the third time he'd seen her since she left five years ago. Always for an hour or two, but Ben could see he was relieved she was there. She was his mother and in her presence it didn't seem to matter that she had disappeared one day when he was six.

"There used to be a couple of Jewish delis in Soho," Ben said. "I don't suppose they are there any more."

"No. I haven't seen them. London's changed so much since you were last there. You should come over for a visit. There's so much for the children to see."

"The guys that ran those delis used to go to Miami for their holidays. I always thought that was strange. Why not go to the South of France?"

"They liked being with their own kind. Like the song says, "A boy like that will kill your brother, stick to your own kind."

"That's from *West Side Story*. I love that play," said Franny. "I'd like to do costumes for it someday."

"I used to do costumes for all the plays at school. That's what got me interested in fashion," said Astrid.

"Mom thinks I should be an actress."

"Follow your heart and you'll be fine."

"You certainly followed yours," said Ben.

"And I'm just fine, aren't I."

"In what category? I'll have lifestyles for ten. Motherhood for one."

"Be nice or I'm leaving. Alex, would you like to spend a month in London with me?"

"Yes."

Ben looked at her.

"You know I wouldn't ask it if I didn't mean it."

"Today."

"Can Franny come too?"

The waitress put the two soups down, leaning in front of Ben to reach Alex. She had the salad as well and returned immediately with four plastic glasses, carried in one hand with her fingers on the rims, four straws, and four drinks in cans clutched tight to her breast.

"Here you go, Luv," she said, sliding a drink over to Alex. "Your hair's gorgeous," she said, touching Astrid's curls. "I'll be right back with the rest of the food."

"Can't wait," Astrid said.

"Mum, do you have a house in London?" Alex asked.

"No. A flat. But a large one in a part of the city known as Worlds End."

"Why?"

"Because it used to be the edge of the city."

"Like Deloraine, Alex. It used to be the City Limits. Although Worlds End, or rather the end of the world was how I thought about it when I was growing up there."

"Here you go, Hon," the waitress said, putting a sandwich special in front of Ben and dealing the other platters.

"Thanks," he said.

"You're welcome, Hon."

He picked up a fry, dipped it into a pool of ketchup, and said, "My doctor put me on a special diet when I was seven. No fries, no ice cream, skim milk only. He thought the fats were upsetting my stomach but it was my parents, not the food I ate."

"See Dad, I'm just like you," Alex said.

"It's true. Only Gemma and I don't fight like my parents."

"That pleasure, Alex, was mine and mine alone," said Astrid.

"I remember," Alex said.

"Mom and Ben don't really fight," Franny said, "they squabble."

"Squabble. Now there's a good descriptive word," said Ben. "You could draw 'squabble.'"

"Are you still drawing?" asked Astrid.

"Every day," Ben said.

"You know, I spoke to a gallery in London about you. The Major Gallery on South Moulton Street."

"Thanks. My time will come."

"So, drawing, teaching, squabbling."

"Plus ça change."

"Anything else?"

"No."

"I don't believe you," she said.

He rolled his eyes in the direction of the children.

"That's it. Except for my role as a father."

"There's something. You have a certain *Je ne sais quoi.*"

"Nothing," he said, and squeezed her thigh below the table.

"I love when you do that," she said, and kissed the side of his face.

"Gross," said Alex.

"Ben, what about Mom?" said Franny.

"We're only fooling around," he said.

"That's how it starts," she said.

There was more talk of London, of double-decker buses and the newly opened Tate Modern and, when the kids were finished eating, Alex asked if they could get some candy at the convenience store in the plaza.

"Sure," Ben said, and gave them each a toonie.

When they were gone he asked Astrid if she meant what she said about Alex coming to visit her.

"Yes," she said. "I'm seeing there might be room in my life now for a child."

"He's not really a child anymore."

"You know what I mean."

"I might need you to take Alex for a while. Could you do it?"

"I think so. He's a sweet boy."

"And he's yours."

"And he's mine. It's not like you to even think like this."

"Give me all your London info."

"Here's my card. Do you have e-mail?"

"Yeah."

The kids came back with long streams of red licorice dangling between their fingers.

She wrote his e-mail address down in the notebook she always carried in her purse. A real pro in spite of her look.

On the way home she sat quietly in the back seat, with her arm around Alex. At Eglinton he leaned his head on her shoulder and closed his eyes.

CHAPTER THIRTY

There was something Alex knew about Astrid even though she had abandoned him. He knew that it wasn't his fault, he knew that in some way she loved him. Seeing her upset him but it also gave him time to be with her. She was his mother and she had never said bad things to him or struck him. She had stayed out for days at a time, but that was another story.

Ben set up a still-life arrangement with a fork and a plate that echoed a photograph Kertesz had taken. It had been two days since his last drawing and he had missed two days before that. Life was getting in the way of art.

Alex was up in his room humming and playing with his old GI Joe toys. He had been bawling in anticipation of seeing Astrid, now he was giddy from the experience. "Mother" was such a loaded concept, with so many expectations, but all anyone knew about Mother was what they had experienced. Ben's was one kind of mother, Astrid was another. In the end she was Alex's mother and, in spite of herself, she was maturing. Ben could see the possibility of there being more contact with her as Alex got older. His needs were changing and his safety and well-being were not the issues they once were. Nice of Astrid to speak to the Major Gallery.

"Dad," Alex said, appearing suddenly at his side, "remember I asked if you could help me make a mobile?"

"Yes."

"Can we do it tomorrow? I need it for Friday."

"Sure. Do you want me to pick you up or do you want to walk down and meet me in the studio?"

"I'll walk," he said.

"Good. Are you alright?"

"About seeing Mom?"

"Yeah."

"I'd forgotten how beautiful and funny she is. Can I really go and visit her in London?"

"I don't see why not."

"Cool."

"Now go to sleep and let me finish this."

"Night, Dad," he said, giving Ben a kiss on the cheek.

"Night, son."

It took him an hour to finish the drawing and when it was done he went up to his office to check his e-mail. There was none. He glanced at the news headlines and, seeking a different kind of distraction, went to claudia'sroom.com. It was eleven o'clock and Kristin Straight was introducing tonight's guest speaker on *The Best Years of Our Lives*, a regular feature of the site.

Kristin was wearing her school uniform.

"Tonight's guest is W," she said, "and she is going to talk about coping with parents who have an active sex life."

Pan to W sitting in a chair in a corner of the room, lit only by a desk lamp on her right side. She was wearing a hooded sweatshirt over a flannel nightgown.

"When I was little my parents used to do it all the time. They would have sex in the living room, the bathroom, the kitchen, the bedroom. Always when they thought I was asleep. When we travelled and shared a room they would wait until it got real late and then do everything. I was often up or woken up and though I tried not to watch, I couldn't help but listen and it was gross. After my two brothers were born things slowed down and eventually my Dad ran away from home and went to Italy, where he fell in love with a girl my age. I thought that was really stupid and told him so. He actually left us to go and be with this girl in Venice. She kicked him out in a week and he came home somewhat ashamed of himself and everything settled down for over a year. I could tell something was wrong with him, though. He was quiet and thoughtful much of the time. He said it was his work. But I didn't believe him.

"I decided to leave Italy and my family and come here for all kinds of reasons and things were going really well until today. Today I had dinner with my Mom who's visiting from Italy. She's been like a saint through all the stuff with my father. Today she told me she's in love with my art teacher. 'Are you fucking him?' I asked, and though she didn't say yes, I knew from the way the colour spread across her cheeks that she was. Well, that's just great. My Mom's fucking my art teacher. He's the only teacher I've ever had who was able to get me working and thinking about art. She's considering moving back to Toronto to be near him. I said, 'Mom, how can you even contemplate that? What about Dad?' And she looked at me, coldly, in a way she never had before and said, 'What about him?' And I must say I knew what she meant. Men are such assholes. My art teacher lives with a woman and their two children. How can he behave so badly? Mom says it goes way back and when I know something about love I'll understand. 'Bullshit,' I said, 'bad behaviour is bad behaviour no matter what you want to call it.' I don't think I can go to art class anymore. I don't think I can stand to look at my teacher. It all makes me so sad I want to cry."

"Thank you, W," Kristen said. "On the next episode of *The Best Years of Our Lives*, M will talk about being spanked by her uncle."

Ben looked at his computer screen in disbelief.

CHAPTER THIRTY-ONE

Arriving at work the next morning he found a copy of
Zoom magazine on his desk. The issue was four years old.

"What's this?" he said to Amanda.

"That new girl, the one that draws really well . . ."

"Wanita?"

"That's right. She left the magazine on your desk, thinking you might want to have a look at it."

The Lazlo Dresh shots of Wanita were marked with a
yellow Post-it. The pictures, pure Dresh, got at the essence
of adolescent sexuality without doing anything obvious or
common. Wanita was fourteen at the time.

There was another Post-it at the end of the series and a
tarty Polaroid of Wanita in a shirt unbuttoned to the waist. A
note read: *"That was then, now is now. In case you hadn't
noticed. And you, silly man, chose my mother instead."*

"One minute we're assholes, the next just silly men."

"What did you say?" Amanda asked.

"Oh, nothing."

He left the office and went to the other end of the studio to call Ellen.

"You told Wanita about us and I think she's jealous and
hurt."

"Don't be silly."

"She was on the Internet last night talking about your dinner and the fact that you are fucking her art teacher. It's a Web site called claudia'sroom.com. Check it out. Look in the archive for the most recent episode of *The Best Years of Our Lives*. She left a copy of *Zoom* magazine on my desk this morning with the Dresh pictures and a note saying she's improved with age and I was stupid to choose her mother."

"This is not the kind of behaviour I would expect from Wanita. And I never said I was fucking you. She asked but I didn't reply."

"You blushed, though, from your neck to your forehead."

"I miss you. Will I see you today?"

"Yes. Are you planning to move back here?"

"Maybe."

"I gotta go. My first class is coming up the stairs."

"I love you."

"I love you too."

It was Wanita's class and she was not there.

Sharon Gold came in the door with the students and he was reminded that he had scheduled a life-drawing class for period one.

"Hi, Sharon."

"Ben."

"Sharon, why don't you get ready and I'll get the students organized for drawing."

He waited for them all to arrive.

"Girls. We have a model today and I thought we'd work in here. Work in the round. So let's push the tables to the side of the room and get set up with easels or drawing boards."

"This is boring. Can't we do something else?"

"This is fundamental."

"Well, can't we get some naked guys around here?"

"Maybe. Everyone take three or four sheets of paper and charcoal."

Sharon came back into the room in her kimono.

Ben described what he wanted to do and she came and stood beside him. There was a chair for one of the poses and she dropped the kimono on that.

"Okay," he said, "five gesture drawings and then a long study."

"How long?"

"Twenty minutes."

"Can we do a longer one?"

"Yeah. The last. It will be thirty."

"Kristen, can I see you for a moment?"

"Sure," she said, leaning her drawing board against the wall.

"Let's talk back here," he said, indicating the small studio.

"Careful, girl," someone shouted out.

She followed him down the narrow hallway.

"Kristen, I know about your Web site and I haven't said anything about it, which is not to say I won't. I think that in some way what you're trying to do is very artful."

"Thanks," she said.

"But I'm concerned about my personal life being made public as it was last night. The intimate workings of people's lives are not meant as entertainment. With what Wanita said, whether it's true or not, a number of people's lives could be affected in a negative and painful way. In a school situation you cannot air gossip and innuendo about the faculty. It's not like there is a big secret about where the site originates from. And when someone says, 'their art teacher,' there is no mystery about who that is in the small world of your audience."

"Not so small."

"What do you mean?"

"Fifty thousand hits a day."

"I think you should close it down."

"I can't do that. I have a responsibility to my viewers."

"With that kind of audience it is inevitable that you will be discovered."

"That's a risk I have to take. I'm a strong believer in freedom of expression and the Internet is the one place where people my age can get our message out."

"It's the nature of your message that concerns me."

"Only because last night happened to be about you. My father used to run into this all the time when he first started his TV station in Jamaica."

Kristen turned away from him then and went back to her drawing.

He had inadvertently supported the Web site by not drawing it to the attention of the administration. When the content affected him personally he asked that it be closed down. This was a kind of censorship and Kristen was right to resist. But was it that straightforward? There was a bigger idea here that seemed to elude him. Thoughts about art and free-expression distracted him throughout his class and into his office afterward. By not forcing Kristen to shut down the Web site he was complicit in its operation. Sharon was standing beside him and bent down to get her day-book to check a date he had proposed for modelling. She wasn't wearing any clothes and when she bent down he looked at her ass. She had flawless skin and there was still a lovely curve to her buttocks.

The door opened then and Wanita cried, "Mr. C! How could you?" and was gone, slamming the door behind her, before he could answer.

"That was really something," Sharon said.

"Yes it was," he said.

"What's with that girl?" Sharon said.

"I don't know," he said.

"Do you still want me tomorrow afternoon?" Sharon asked.

"Yes," he said.

CHAPTER THIRTY-TWO

⊙⊙

He opened the window after Sharon left, allowing in a rush of cold October air.

Suki Jacobs, in tenth grade, tapped on the metallic office door with her skull-and-crossbones ring.

"What is it?"

"Sir," she said, stepping into the room, "the whole class is here. What do you want us to do?"

"Run through the science corridor naked and see if anyone notices."

"And besides that?"

"Work on your etchings. Take out the tools and I'll set up the acid bath."

"What if we're finished?"

"Sign and number the prints and hand them in."

"That should take all of five minutes. Then what?"

"You can do a wild print. On a plate use anything but an etching tool to make marks on it. Take it outside, up to the Village, stand on it, drag it along the road, it doesn't matter."

"That sounds like fun. Can I use a big plate?"

"Sure."

He adjusted the window and re-arranged the things on his desk before going out to his class.

"Sir, are you alright?" one of them asked.

"Yeah, why?"

"You look a little pale."

"I'm fine," he said.

"I need the acid."

"Me too."

"Why can't we get it ourselves?"

"This is such a waste of time."

"I need edition paper."

"I'll cut some," he said, unlocking the cupboard where the acid was kept. "When I finish this."

The phone rang. He had the gallon jug of nitric acid solution in his hands. If it was important the caller would leave a message. One of the kids answered it though and another grabbed it out of her hand.

"Hello, art room," she said. ". . . May I tell him who's calling? . . . Sir, it's for you. A friend."

He carefully poured the nitric acid into a tray and turned on the fan for the slot hood. Then took the phone and stepped out onto the landing.

"Hello," he said.

"You bastard. How could you?"

"What?"

"Don't what me. Wanita told me about you fucking some model in your office. You're despicable. I had your cock in my mouth yesterday. Where had it been before that? You men are all pigs. Pigs."

"Sir, what about that paper?"

"Just a second."

"Has it occurred to you she might be lying? Making all this up? I told you this morning she was upset. Last night

I was fucking her mother and today I'm fucking some model up the ass?"

"Well, you are fucking her mother."

"I didn't fuck any model. Believe me. When did she say this happened?"

"This morning."

"Right. I regularly make a habit of fucking models in my office between classes."

"I don't know what to believe."

"I love you. You love me. That's all."

"I'm so confused. Listening to Wanita on that Web site broke my heart. But the other stuff. I called Patricia Post and really gave her a piece of my mind. I asked how a school like St. Simon's could allow its students to broadcast obscenity on the Internet."

"And what did she say?"

"She said she didn't know anything about it and that she would look into it."

"Great."

"Call me when you finish," she said.

CHAPTER THIRTY-THREE

In the Village there was a Japanese place where he could get a bowl of noodles. He liked the owners and went there for lunch after class. He was worried about Ellen's phone call to Miss Post. He had the spicy noodles and a salad and talked about the state of public education, the difficulties with quitting smoking and the Argos' chances of winning the Grey Cup. There was a big picture window and he watched the people on the street. It was a pleasant distraction. Back at school he found a note in his mail box requesting a meeting in the Head's office at one-fifteen and both the receptionist and Miss Post's personal secretary reminded him not to be late. There was a message on his phone and an e-mail as well. He wondered if they had called his parents. What if he hadn't come back? He had the next period free. What if he had gone for a walk, or had another cup of coffee? He had forgotten the new rule that all members of the faculty were required to sign in and out when they entered or left the building and that all faculty were required to be available from eight-thirty a.m. until four-thirty p.m. It was the new management strategy — get the place ship-shape and off-load the slackers.

He took his time getting to Miss Post's office. She was not alone. On her right sat Miss Marconi, a vice-principal, imported from the States, who never failed to remind people that her ancestors came over on the *Mayflower* with Benedict Arnold. And on her left sat lovely Penelope Rivers, also a vice-principal, with legs like willow branches and breasts that could make a grown man cry. He smiled at Penelope but she looked at him without expression. Only the blood in her pale cheeks let him know the severity of the moment. He was not invited to sit down.

"Mr. Calder, what is going on here? Just what in the hell is going on?" said Miss Post, half sitting, half standing, hardly able to contain herself.

"I'm sorry," he said, "I don't know what you are talking about."

"Mr. Calder," she said, "do you know the Web site called claudia'sroom?"

"Yes, I do."

"And how long have you known about it?"

"For a few weeks. One of the students alerted me to its existence."

"Now Mr. Calder, why didn't you inform the administration of this Web site with its disgusting pornographic images of our students, emanating from our residence?"

"I was curious to see where it was going and I didn't think it was at all pornographic. There were some graphic images but nothing worse than you see in the magazines the kids read. There were also some moving and informed vignettes."

"Mr. Calder, your behaviour around this issue is reprehensible. It shows absolutely no concern for the reputation of our school. Surely you can't abide having details of your personal life discussed so publicly by students, students who are making the most serious allegations against you?"

"They could be making it up, couldn't they? A kind of performance art. I know the girl who runs the site has higher goals than mere gossip and titillation. It's empowering for her to have a voice."

"Kristen Straight, Mr. Calder, has been expelled. She will be on the first plane back to Jamaica. I can't believe you are still trying to protect her. Where are your brains, Mr. Calder?"

"Funny you should ask," he said, undoing his pants and exposing himself to the tribunal.

"I think that's enough, Mr. Calder," Miss Post said, as she stood up and pushed her chair back behind her. Once again she had a gold-tipped fountain pen in her hand but this time she held it like a dagger and he doubted she would throw it. Meeting his eye she set the pen down on the table. "You can put your pants on and leave this building immediately."

"Does that mean I'm fired or is it just a temporary suspension?"

"It means you're fired, you idiot."

"You will, of course, be hearing from my lawyer," he said, bending to pull up his pants.

"Goodbye, Mr. Calder."

He went up to his office to get his jacket and his binder and to tell Amanda what happened. She was teaching a class and had to sit down when he said he had been fired. They had worked together for twenty years.

"Here's the key to my filing cabinet," he said. "There is some art in the bottom drawer that students have given me over time. Can you pack it in a box and drop it off at my place?"

"Yes. Anything else?"

"No. That's all I want. I'll tell you what happened when I see you."

He left the studio and saw Wanita on the landing leading to the residence. She was just standing there looking distraught, agitated. She had dark circles under her eyes and her hair was tied down with a bandana.

"I liked you very much," she said, "as a teacher and as a man and I thought the feeling was mutual. I saw how you looked at me and there was that easy flow of conversation."

"I do like you. And you're Ellen's daughter. We could be friends forever but not around here. I just got fired."

"God, I'm sorry. I didn't want this to happen."

"It's alright. I won't say you didn't behave badly but I certainly don't hold it against you. This isn't your fault."

"What about my art work? Who will replace you?"

"I don't know. It doesn't matter. I'll always be available for you."

"What's my mother got that I don't?"

"She and I have a history that goes back to when we were young."

"Well, I don't want you living together," she said, and burst out crying.

He put his arms around her and hugged her.

It was then that the tribunal found him.

"If you don't want to be charged with sexual assault I suggest you leave now," Miss Post said.

"We'll talk later," he said, releasing Wanita, but she didn't want to be released and clung to his arm.

"You were wrong for expelling Kristin," she said, wiping her nose with her sleeve. "We all made that Web site."

"And you will all be put on disciplinary probation," said Miss Marconi.

"The students hate you," Wanita said.

"Be careful young lady or you will be next," said Miss Post.

"You think I care?"

"We understand how upset you are," Miss Marconi offered.

"Fuck you," Wanita said, and turned into the residence.

"Good job, ladies."

"Get out, Mr. Calder. Now."

CHAPTER THIRTY-FOUR

⊙⦵⊙

Ben went to see Ellen. Her father was sitting out in the driveway, in his wheelchair, getting some sun, with the Philippino caregiver at his side. His hair was white and long and he smiled with a distinct pleasure as Ben approached, twisting his right hand like it held the throttle of a motorcycle. Ben touched his knuckles with his own. The front door was open. Ben stepped into the foyer and called Ellen's name.

"I look like shit," she said, coming out of the den. "It always ends the same way with you. I look and feel like shit."

"End, what do you mean, end?"

"I'm going home. Why would I trade one philandering bastard for another. At least I know Casey's limitations. With you, it's a big unknown."

"What are you talking about?"

"That girl this morning."

"I thought we were over that. I told you I didn't fuck anyone. Wanita made it up. Ask her. I just got fired. And it's your fault."

"Mine. How so?"

"You alerted Miss Post to claudia'sroom."

"Well, you should have. There was some disturbing stuff on there. I certainly don't need to think of my daughter's classmate peeling a banana and sticking it in her roommate's vagina then eating it and calling it the 'Tuesday Breakfast Segment.' As a teacher and a member of the community you had an obligation."

"Maybe, but as an artist I thought Kristen Straight had a right to take it as far as she wanted and it wasn't my job to shut it down."

"Artist. Shmartist. You and Casey think you can excuse any aberrant behaviour in the name of Art. Art is nothing. It's like exercise or dieting or renovating a house."

"No. Art is all that endures."

"Oh Ben, look at your life. What have you got to show for it? Nothing. You're piss poor because of art. Now you don't even have a job. Look around. You're almost fifty and you're a big fucking loser."

"I've got you."

"No you don't. You've always been a loser with some irresistible charm but I'm looking for a man who is grounded. I'm looking for a man who will think about me first and my pussy second."

"My instincts about you were right. Even as a teenager I knew you were just a straight chick who would never understand what my struggle in life was all about."

"Your struggle was all about getting laid. And I think it still is."

"Sex is the undercurrent. Without it, life is stagnant."

"Grow up, Ben. What are you going to do when your body begins to decline? To fail you? Look at my Dad."

"I'll pray that my mind goes as well. If it doesn't, I'll have to learn to live on a higher plane. That's where art and meditation will come in. That or heroin."

"Stop kidding around. This is serious. I love you yet I'm willing to walk away. That should tell you something."

"It tells me you're afraid and you have an iron will. I love you. What I feel for you transcends any ideas or thoughts about compatibility. It's very pure this ache I feel for you."

"I know," she said.

"Don't go," he said.

"Make love to me," she said, taking his hand and leading him up to her bedroom.

There were two single beds with pink satin covers. They lay down on one of them surrounded by a collection of dolls, in fancy dresses and crinolines, stuffed animals and pictures of her water skiing and the trophies she had won competing.

At four-thirty he looked at his watch.

"I gotta go," he said.

"What's the rush?"

"Alex. I was supposed to meet him in the art studio after school. He was walking down alone for the first time and he was very proud."

"He'll be alright."

"What if they say, 'Your father doesn't work here any more,' and turn him away? He'll panic."

"Like you are now."

"Yeah."

It's true, he was panicking. Like those times when Alex was little and Ben would lose sight of him in a store at the mall. Now he was desperate to find him.

"I'm leaving tomorrow at five," Ellen said.

He raced through the narrow residential streets to St. Simon's and pulled into the front driveway. Leaving the motor running he ran in looking for Alex on one of the benches in the entrance hall. When he didn't see him he continued running up the stairs. Alex was not there, nor had he been according to the two students who were work-ing on a project.

Marija, the late-shift receptionist, met him at the bot-tom of the stairs.

"Your son was here," she said.

"Where is he now?"

"I don't know. I told him you went home."

"Thanks."

"I'm sorry about what happened."

He got in the car and peeled out of the driveway.

Alex didn't have a key. Would he go home or back to school?

Ben figured Alex would go home and that's where he went as well. Driving fast along St. Clair and down Avenue Road. He made the left at Roxborough, pushing his way through rush-hour traffic to honking horns and drivers giv-ing him the finger.

"Fuck you too," he shouted.

The house was dark and he didn't see Alex when he stopped the car, but as he ran up the stairs he saw his feet. Alex was sitting, with his arms around his knees, partially hidden by the big bush in front of the porch.

"Oh, am I glad to see you," Ben said, sitting down and giving him a hug.

"Dad, where were you?" Alex said, shrinking away from him.

"It's been an unusual day. I'm sorry. This has never hap-pened before."

"And it better not happen again. I was scared and didn't know what to do. I called your cellphone but you hadn't turned it on."

"I didn't even have it with me. I'll get you a phone and we'll keep the lines opened always."

"I don't want a phone. Then I'll be like those kids at my school calling their parents all the time. They make me sick. They call from class when they forget their homework and their mothers and sometimes their fathers drive it over. The kids order them around."

"Maybe it's time to leave the Village," Ben said.

"Maybe. But where would I go? I still have friends there."

"England. France. Italy."

"Oh Dad, stop joking around. What about the mobile? I need it for tomorrow."

"Listen, son. I lost my job today. That's why I wasn't there."

"Well, you must be happy. After all the complaining you've done."

"It's not that simple. I've got to figure out a way to make some money."

"Like what?" Alex said.

"I don't know. In twenty years it's the only job I've had."

"Dad. My tummy hurts."

"It's just nerves. Look, I still have enough money to get you a treat. Let's walk over to Patachou and we'll work on the mobile after."

"What about Franny?"

"I'll take my cellphone in case she calls. She had a soccer practice after school."

"Don't forget to turn it on."

"Thanks. I won't."

Inside, the kitchen phone started to ring.

It was Gemma calling to say she'd be working late. "When do you think you'll be home?" he asked.

"I don't know. We have to finish this scene tonight. Our permit for the location has expired."

"Are you okay?"

"Yeah, a little tired and a little cold," she said. "You?"

"I'm fine."

"Did you remember Franny has a birthday party at Rosalind Klein's house?"

"No. I remembered the soccer game but not the party."

"You have to pick her up at nine-thirty. Sixteen Dunbar. It's on the calendar."

"Sixteen. Okay. See you later."

"Don't wait up for me."

"Yeah."

"It's just us," he said to Alex, pushing the hair from in front of his eyes. "Why don't you put a jacket on? It'll be cold on the way home."

"I'm fine," said Alex, holding his father's hand.

CHAPTER THIRTY-FIVE

Wanita called him late on Friday night. Gemma and the kids were asleep and he was drawing and drinking, far into his second bottle of wine.

"Hi," she said. "I didn't know if you'd be up. I was going to leave a message if you didn't answer."

"I'm here. I usually go to sleep quite late."

"I miss Mom," she said.

"Me too."

"I thought maybe we could get together. I've got some drawings I want to show you."

"Sure."

"How about tomorrow?"

"According to the calendar my afternoon looks pretty free. Do you want to come over here?"

"That sounds okay."

"I can't pick you up, though. I sold my car."

"Well, maybe we could meet somewhere."

"How about that Italian café in the Village."

"I've never been there, but sure. How could you part with that old car?"

"Easy. I need the money and one of the crew members on Gemma's film was anxious to have it. How's two tomorrow?"

"Okay. They hired a new art teacher. A woman. Miss Divorak."

"Frizzy black hair, about thirty-five?"

"Yes."

"We met at a conference. I think she knows what she's doing."

"She seems nice. Miss Post knew her from her old school and remembered she was on a leave this year."

"I guess they made her an offer she couldn't refuse."

"I'd want billions to teach in a place like this."

"It's not so bad."

"Kristen is starting a new Web site. It premieres on Monday and she is soliciting pieces from all of us. Maybe you want to contribute something."

"I don't think so."

"Okay. Well. I'll see you tomorrow."

"Bye."

He hung up the phone and continued with his drawing.

Ten minutes later, around one in the morning, Ellen called from Italy.

"Hi," she said.

"Hi."

"I miss you."

"Me too."

"How are you doing?"

"I don't know. Alright, I guess. I sold my car yesterday. I got five-thousand dollars for it. That should last a couple of months."

"What are you going to do?"

"I don't know. There aren't any teaching jobs around and I'm not a candidate for a good letter of recommendation. I'll do some portfolio consulting for kids who want to go into fine art or architecture. A few parents have already been in touch with me."

"That sounds positive."

"The climate around drawing seems to be changing too, so I might take my work out and try to get a show."

"It's certainly good enough."

"It all depends on someone thinking they can sell it and that's never been the case before. How are you? How was your flight?"

"The flight was uneventful. It was good to get home and see the boys. Casey is still withdrawn and not being up front about why. He was happy to see Wanita's drawing of me though. And I can't get you out of my mind. I keep flashing on moments we had and I want them again."

"I feel the same way. What are you wearing?" he asked.

"My dressing gown. It's seven in the morning here."

"Where's your husband?"

"He went out for a walk."

"Where are you?"

"I'm sitting on my bed. With pillows propped up behind my back."

"What do you see?"

"A meadow, the walls of Montefiorelle, some farm houses and the rolling hills of Chianti off in the distance. The church bell just rang seven times. The sky is slightly overcast with patches of blue breaking through."

"It sounds so peaceful."

"It is quite magical. Compared to Cottingham Street it's like living in a dream. What are you doing?"

"I'm sitting at the table, drawing."

"What?"

"Two lemons and an eggplant."

"What's the weather like?"

"It's a cold October night."

"My window is opened wide and there's a fragrant breeze coming in off the meadow. The air is like a whisper on my skin. I feel waves of desire."

"I can smell you and taste you."

"Stop. What are your plans for today?"

"We promised the kids pizza and a movie. And before that, I'm meeting Wanita. She called earlier. There are some drawings she wants to show me."

"Is she alright?"

"As far as I can tell. I'll let you know when I see her. What are you doing later?"

"Not much. Some friends are coming over for dinner. They have boys the same age as ours. Casey built a soccer goal in the field behind the house and the kids play two-on-two for hours at a time. He's back. I'll call you on Sunday," Ellen said.

"Call my cellphone."

"Okay. I love you."

"Why aren't you here?"

"Bye."

"Yeah."

He finished the drawing and the bottle of wine, turned out the lights and lay down on the sofa. Gemma was angry with him for getting fired. She thought his defence of Kristen and her Web site was stupid and that he was turning into another middle-aged man happy for any opportunity to see young women cavorting around in the nude.

And she was worried and concerned about money as well. It didn't matter that he had supported her through the doldrums of her career. Now that she was working again she didn't want him living off her earnings. She'd been there before and didn't want to do it again. In her mind, a man financially dependent on a woman was bound to become miserable and abusive.

He lay in the dark, numb from the wine, but not numb enough. It was the first time in twenty years he'd been without a steady source of income and he too was scared. He'd always taken the money for granted. Now what?

Gemma shook him awake in the morning.

"We've been invited out to the country, for the day," she said, "and I'd like to go."

"I feel like shit."

"You had too much to drink, but that's another story."

"What about pizza and a movie?"

"We can do that tomorrow after the soccer finals."

"Whose place?"

"A friend of Walter's. It's in Caledon on the Credit River. You could go fishing. The guy's an artist. I thought you might like him and he's really well connected. His name is Norton Hammish."

"I know Norton Hammish and I don't want to spend ten minutes with him."

"You're always so judgmental. We never meet anyone new."

"Norton Hammish was fucking Astrid for three months before we split up. We were friends. He's a prick. An arrogant prick at that."

"That was then. This is now."

"I saw him two weeks ago. He's still a prick."

"Well, I'm going to go. Walter has a daughter Franny's age and his wife is in town for the weekend. We all thought it would be fun to get together. I'll take the kids. They arranged for a limo to pick us up at eleven."

"You have fun."

"I will."

"Hey, Hammish and I have a history. I just lost my job. I have no visibility as an artist. I just don't feel like hanging out with all the winners today."

"Fine, you stay here and feel sorry for yourself."

"Fuck you."

"Fuck you too."

CHAPTER THIRTY-SIX

"The limo's here, Dad."

"Well, you have fun and I'll see you when you get back."

"Promise."

"Of course. What do you think?"

"I don't know."

He gave Alex a hug but he didn't go downstairs. He just waved at Gemma and Franny through the window. When they were gone he showered and had breakfast. At one-thirty he left the house to meet Wanita.

He walked past Ellen's old house on Cottingham. It was one of the houses in the city he liked but could never afford. There was an arched window in the front and a long solid wall of brick facing the laneway that felt vaguely European. It was a sunny day, with a clear autumn sky. The leaves on the big maples had turned to yellow ochre and brown with the occasional flash of red. From Russell Hill Road he cut through Winston Churchill Park to Spadina. The air was clean and vibrant, like mountain air with an abundance of positive ions and he was rising to the occasion of such a fine day, moving up through the levels of alcohol-induced darkness to connect with the moment.

Dogs ran free in the park with their owners, talking in groups, swinging little bags of shit from their hands. Others hit balls out over the valley and the dogs chased after them, running down and up the steep hills. It was a long way to go and the dogs did it time and time again.

The playground was full of children and people were playing tennis. It was more like a summer day than one so close to November. He crossed the running path and continued up Spadina, past Heath and St. Simon's, toward Forest Hill Village. It was like England, this commercial crossroads in the middle of a residential community and it was jumping with kids on skateboards and bikes and adults in form fitting clothes on roller blades. Gone was the blue-rinse crowd in their Cadillac Fleetwood sedans.

He saw Wanita walking toward him. Like Ellen, she owned her body, possessed it and filled it from the inside. When she reached him they hugged on the street and kissed each other on both cheeks. She was carrying a roll of drawings in her hand.

"The way you move," he said, "I thought you were Ellen."

"Usually I wouldn't want to hear that. I've heard it all my life. But today it's okay," she said, linking her arm with his as they turned toward the Portofino coffee bar.

It was in the middle of the block and had a few tables outside. All seats were occupied by people animated in conversation, smoking and enjoying the sun. Ben and Wanita went inside. A lovely old-fashioned mural of Portofino harbour ran the length of one wall.

"Have you been there?" he asked.

"No, we were going to go for a weekend then Dad freaked out about something and it was cancelled."

"The original Monte Carlo pizzeria on Eglinton had a mural like this. After twenty years they covered it up and it became a *ristorante* with a dress code. Then they went broke. What do you want to have?"

"I'll have a latte. I never saw a *ristorante* in Italy."

"It's a Toronto thing. I think it means, 'no dining pleasure.'"

He ordered an espresso, a latte and a salami sandwich. They sat on the long banquette that ran under the mural.

"I spoke to your mother last night. She called about ten minutes after you did. She wants you to know she is thinking about you and misses you very much."

"I miss her too. It was like we got to a new level when she was here. More intimate. More like girlfriends. When she told me she loved you, I hated that she was deceiving Dad but I knew that he had not exactly been innocent. Is this what all adults do?"

"Not all."

"Well, I think it sucks, and if my husband was screwing around on me I'd cut his balls off with a pair of scissors."

The coffees and his sandwich were ready and he picked them up at the counter.

"I remember our first conversation at Salerno. It was what, three weeks ago?"

"You wanted me that day. I could tell. There was a little spark when we touched."

"I didn't want you. I thought you were very attractive but I didn't want you."

"Liar. The girls all talk about how you lust after them."

"It's a fantasy. Boarding school does strange things to a girl's mind. You have a hundred girls between thirteen and nineteen and not a boy in sight. It's an opportunity for the imagination to run wild."

"At night, Kristen, Janine, Helen, and I used to lie on the floor, in a circle, with our feet touching in the centre and talk about people we wanted to have sex with. You were the only male teacher that could hold our interest long enough."

"Long enough for what?"

"You know."

"And females?"

"The most desired was that piano teacher from Russia."

"Miss Gochenko."

"Yes."

"She held my interest for a short time. She's like the only faculty member with an idea of how to get dressed when she gets up in the morning. Her boyfriend plays hockey for an NHL team in the States, and the money she doesn't spend on clothes she sends home to her mother in Odessa."

"It's always been hard to think about teachers having lives outside of school."

"Let's see your drawings."

"In a minute. These are an experiment. I saw this girl's work in *Art in America* and thought I'd try something like it."

"Let's see," he said.

"Oh, alright."

They were all compressed charcoal on newsprint. The first image depicted Wanita, nude, from the floor up. There was foreshortening and a compression of the body. The second was her sitting on a stool but from the same point of view. The third showed her kneeling.

"Jenny Saville. She's British, and did a series of nude self-portraits. Very large format, from odd angles, in a lovely muted palette, and her eye absolutely clear and focused. Like yours. There is no sentimentality here. No cheap emotion. No attempt to idealize your body. Your aim, as they say, is true."

"So you like them."

"Very much."

In the fourth drawing she was lying on her side with her back to the mirror, looking over her shoulder; in the fifth she was on all fours drawing her body from the neck to the hips, and in the last she was kneeling on one knee.

"They each took about two hours."

"I can see the concentration. They're strong and make a real impression on the picture space. I'd like to see you working larger than this. Maybe 4' x 5'. Pick one pose and try to do it large."

"In charcoal?"

"Yeah. Or in paint."

"I don't know how to paint."

"You could use a black wash or find a range of colours that work together and apply them with the same light and dark values as in a drawing. I'll help you."

"How much would you charge."

"You, nothing."

"I'd want to pay. After all, you are out of a job."

"What I would charge isn't going to save me from imminent poverty. These are powerful. You have something and should be given every opportunity to develop."

"I'll talk to Mom. See what she says."

"Okay."

She rolled up the drawings and they went out onto the street. The sun was shining directly in their faces. They could both feel the heat.

"God, it's a beautiful day," he said.

She put her arm in his and they started walking north on Spadina. At Coulson they crossed the road and went into the park.

They continued walking through the park, past the nannies on benches talking quietly to each other while their charges played on the slide. There were some elderly couples as well, and a few teenagers sitting on the ground smoking and listening to music. At the end of the park they followed the path through a small forest out into a broad grassy ravine. It was the bottom of Glenayr, the street he had lived on as a teenager but he hadn't spent much time down here. There hadn't been any reason. It was a wild place, swampy and dense with vegetation.

Now there was a path through it that went from Heath almost to Eglinton. It was usually busy with runners, cyclists and people out for a stroll. Today it was unusually quiet. Maybe it was the time of day, half-past three, and the season. It would be getting dark soon and nobody wanted to be down there after dark. When they got to the Bathurst Bridge, the bridge Andrew Feldman had jumped to his death from, Wanita said she had to pee, she had to pee really bad. It was all that coffee. And before he could say anything, she took a few steps off the path, undid her jeans, pulling them and her under pants down below her thighs, then squatted and peed, the sound like a faucet running on the hard ground under the bridge.

"You wouldn't have a Kleenex?" she said.

"No, but you could use this," he said, offering an old bandana from his jacket pocket.

She wiped herself with it and stood up.

"You keep it."

"No thanks," she said, and tossed it.

Her pants were still down.

"You want to touch it, don't you?"

"Yes," he said, overcome with desire.

"Well you can't. You chose my mother."

"Let me," he said, taking her shoulders in his hands, then kneeling down pressing his face into her dark mound.

"You're truly disgusting," she said, and tried to pull away but he held her by the hips, his fingers digging into her buttocks.

Frightened, she hit the side of his face with her hand and kicked him hard in the groin. He groaned and let go, collapsing like a punctured membrane, and she pulled up her jeans and ran back on the path toward the park.

She had caught the side of his nose when she hit him and he was bleeding and lying folded up in a fetal ball, his shoulder in the puddle of her urine. The spirits of Andrew Feldman and all the other jumpers squealed around him. He could see the imprints where they fell. He was not close to dead but he couldn't move. His life, as he knew it, was over. Only Alex's voice, tugging at him until well after dark, got him to stand up and leave that place. Near the top of a steep hill, behind the Heath Street subway entrance, a block from St. Simons, he stopped to catch his breath with the homeless who had gathered there, seeking shelter from the imminent storm. The temperature had dropped suddenly and there was talk of ice and snow. It all had to do with the wind.

At home Alex recoiled from the sight of him.

"You stink," he said, "and you lied."

EPILOGUE

Gemma and Franny moved into Norton Hammish's studio until the film was finished and she could find a place of her own. With what remained of his money Ben took Alex to London where they stayed with Astrid in her large Worlds End flat. He left everything behind on Roxborough, except his drawings. Astrid and Alex began to grow close and he had the pleasure of living with both his parents, in relative harmony, for a short period of time. Astrid paid for him to go to school and dressed him like a prince. The Mayor Gallery agreed to represent Ben's work and give him a one-man show in a year's time. He and Ellen spoke on the phone. She was reluctant at first but she could not cut him loose. Against her husband's wishes she met Ben for a weekend in Paris. All around them, fear crept through the city's streets, and reason, backed up on its haunches, trembled in dark corners.

Acknowledgements

Thanks to the gang at EXILE, Michael Callaghan, Nina Callaghan and especially Barry Callaghan without whose continued support and enthusiasm my work would remain unpublished. Thanks to Claire Weissman Wilks for critiquing the visuals. Thanks to Bernice Eisenstein for her good input and advice on this one, and Carolyn Zeifman for her insight. Sarah Agnew for her clear vision and her capacity to spend a part of each day with me. The boys of course, Clancy, Emmett, Jesse and Michelle for her good will.